NO MATCH FOR A TEXAN

"Let it drop, hombre!" commanded the black-clad Texan, his voice a pleasant tenor that nonetheless had a hard and a somehow chillingly savage note.

Turning as he heard the words, shortest of the group and thickset, McAvoy gave no indication of being willing to comply. Filled with the kind of hatred all his kind had for Southrons, he was disinclined to obey. But before McAvoy could turn his snub-nosed Webley Bulldog revolver up, he saw the black-clad Texan moving his way . . .

*   Denotes title awaiting publication.
( )   Denotes position in which a proposed title will be placed.

WEDGE GOES TO ARIZONA

J. T. Edson

A DELL BOOK

Published by
Dell Publishing
a division of
Bantam Doubleday Dell Publishing Group, Inc.
1540 Broadway
New York, New York 10036

The trademark Dell® is registered in the U.S. Patent and
Trademark Office.

ISBN: 0-440-22218-4

Printed in the United States of America

Published simultaneously in Canada

August 1996

10 9 8 7 6 5 4 3 2 1
RAD

*To all those denizens of my "spiritual" home, the
Half Moon in Melton Mowbray, who have endured my
lousy jokes. As proof of my undying gratitude,
if any of you should want an autographed copy of
this book, go out and buy a copy. Then I will be
only too delighted to oblige. There's generous
for you, as my friends from Wales would put it.*

Author's Note

When supplying us with the information from which we produce our books, one of the strictest rules imposed upon us by the present-day members of what we call the "Hardin, Fog and Blaze" clan and the "Counter" family is that we *never* under *any* circumstances disclose their true identity or their present locations. Furthermore, we are instructed to always employ enough inconsistencies with regard to periods and places in which incidents take place to ensure neither can happen even inadvertently.

We would also point out that the names of people who appear in this volume are those supplied to us by our informants in Texas, and any resemblance with those of other persons, living or dead, is purely coincidental.

To save our "old hands" repetition, but for the benefit of new readers, we have given "potted biographies" of Captain Dustine Edward Marsden "Dusty" Fog, Mark Counter, and the Ysabel Kid in the form of Appendixes.

We realize that, in our present permissive society, we could use the actual profanities employed by various people in the narrative. However, we do not concede that a spurious desire to create "realism" is any justification for doing so.

We refuse to pander to the current trendy usage of the metric system, except that when referring to the caliber of certain firearms traditionally measured in millimeters—i.e., Luger 9mm—we will continue to employ miles, yards, feet, inches, pounds, and ounces when quoting distances and weights.

Lastly, and of the *greatest* importance, we must stress that the attitudes and speech of the characters are put down as would have been the case at the period of this narrative.

J. T. EDSON
MELTON MOWBRAY
Leics.,
England

1
NOW COMES THE *TRICKY* PART!

Even in prehistoric times, before man had domesticated such animals for his use, it had been discovered that herbivorous creatures that lived in herds could be induced to move in a desired direction when necessary. With the development of agriculture, which made depending for a living on hunting unnecessary, the knowledge was put to good use when there was a need to move one's livestock from place to place. Because of dire necessity, the technique had been brought to its highest state of development in America during the years following the War Between the States.

Left practically unchecked throughout the four years of the conflict and well able to cope without the close human supervision required by more domesticated breeds, the half-wild longhorn cattle in Texas had grown until vast numbers roamed the open range. Men with vision such as Colonel Charles Goodnight,[1] his partner, Oliver Loving, Jesse Chisholm, Abel Head "Shangai" Pierce, and General Jackson Baines "Ole Devil" Hardin—although Hardin had been confined to a wheelchair following a serious riding accident and had been prevented from participating at first hand with his OD Connected ranch's drives[2]—had seen how this could help them recover from the dire financial straits that had arisen from their support of the Confederate States. At first, the only markets had been the hide and tallow factories; their prices were never higher than four dollars a head, with calves required to be included free. Realizing that such sales would not solve the very serious monetary problems they were facing, the same men had sought and found other outlets.[3]

The most important of the new sources for disposing of the herds were the intercontinental railroads, which offered a speedy means to take the cattle to the already heavily populated and meat-hungry Eastern states. However, before such a potential source of wealth could be exploited, the animals had to be delivered to the shipping points offered by the various towns that grew up along the tracks in Kansas. Despite the extremely long distances involved, especially from the southern parts of Texas, this had not proved insurmountable. Soon herds were flowing north in ever-increasing numbers and the skills of the men taking them were developed to a degree that many cowhands from the Lone Star State became expert in performing the various tasks required on the journey.[4]

* * *

Sitting his fifteen-hand *bayos-cebrunos* gelding selected from his mount—no Texan used the word "string" for the horses rotated in use for his work—in the *remuda* in a relaxed posture—but maintaining himself the straight-backed posture imbued during his training at West Point prior to having left and served with distinction as an officer, rising to the rank of captain with Hood's Texas Brigade in the Confederate States Cavalry through the Civil War— Martin Jethro "Stone" Hart studied what was happening to his rear with a sense of satisfaction arising from a belief that all was going well. In his early thirties, he was handsome apart from a livid white scar caused by a slash from a Yankee saber running down the length of his otherwise tanned right cheek.[5] He was just over six feet tall, and there was a suggestion of whipcord power to his slender frame. Regardless of his being the owner and trail boss of what he intended on arrival to start calling his Wedge Ranch, he wore the attire of a working cowhand, which showed signs that he did not merely supervise but had already helped handle the cattle he was now watching.

Sitting alongside his employer, with whom he had served as a sergeant major while "wearing the gray" in the War Between the States, Standish "Waggles" Harrison also experienced a sensation of well-being. He was around ten years older than Stone, matching Stone in height but more heavily built without being bulky. His hair and mustache were turning gray and his deeply bronzed rugged features were their usual expressionless mask. His clothing was that of a working cowhand and also indicative of his not having restricted himself to overseeing the rest of the crew in his capacity of *segundo*. Whereas his boss carried an ivory-handled Colt on a rig allowing it to be withdrawn swiftly, and could utilize its full potential if required, Waggles, admitting a lack of such skill, wore his—with standard factory walnut grips and the seven-and-a-half-inch Cavalry Model barrel—butt forward for a low-twist hand draw.

Because they had been together for so long and had shared so many perilous situations, the *segundo* could generally tell what his boss was thinking. At that moment, Stone was musing upon how this trail drive was not like any other they had made since taking up the task when deciding it offered them a better means of livelihood than anything else available in Texas at that time.

The methods being employed for keeping the animals

moving were the same, but the herd that was wending a
leisurely way across an area of rolling, predominantly open
country in the warmth of an early-spring afternoon was
traveling westward, not in the northerly direction required
to reach the railroad shipping towns in Kansas. Furthermore, previously the cattle had belonged to ranchers who
lacked sufficient stock or the money necessary to cover the
costs and still show a worthwhile profit. This time, all the
animals were Stone's property and carried the Wedge
brand, which previously was only added to whatever mark
of ownership was borne prior to moving out. Nor were they
intended for sale immediately on arrival at their destination. Rather, they were to add to the nucleus of stock on a
ranch from which marketable herds would be produced.
For this reason, such calves as were born were kept instead
of being disposed of as an encumbrance to the pace that
could be maintained with only grown animals and, as far as
was possible, mainly steers.

While the longhorns that had been the source of wealth
for Texas predominated in the herd, there was a significant
number of the already predominantly red and white breed
known as Hereford cattle originally imported from Great—
as it was then—Britain in 1817 by Henry Clay, a landowner
in Kentucky. From this small beginning of a bull, a cow, and
heifer, the strain had gradually become popular in the East
by virtue of its meat's quality and its milk-producing capacity. The progress was slower west of the Mississippi River;
the majority of ranchers there knew that the greater ease
by which longhorns could proliferate with a minimum need
for human supervision made them a better proposition.

Nevertheless, by the time of the present drive, Herefords
were being raised in increasing numbers by forward-
thinking cattlemen as offering a more substantial return
when sold due to their providing a grade of beef superior to
that from their free-ranging and at best only semidomesti-

cated predecessors, whose way of life was not conducive to the cultivation of tender flesh. With a natural-born conservatism, many cowhands and not a few cattlemen damned the "new" stock as being too delicate to be allowed to range free and lacking the natural instincts to survive while doing so, which came instinctively to longhorns as a result of their only very rarely having been granted constant care and attention through countless generations.[6] On the other hand, forward-thinking men of influence in the cattle business had gained faith in the "Limey critters," and Stone, although he could not claim to be one of their number because his connection with the business was confined to his role as a successful trail boss handling other people's stock, was willing to be guided by them now that he was to be engaged in raising stock on his own account.

Winding across the rolling plains country, the cattle were being kept moving by riders spaced along each side of the column. Those at the head of the line—on the "point"— were responsible for keeping the animals following the directions of the trail boss or his *segundo*, whoever was currently riding a short distance in front. Covering the first third of the line were the men designated as being on the "swing." The "flank" men were positioned along the next third, and the rear was brought up by the cowhands riding the "drag."

Although usually only two at most would be used, off to one side at the head of the column were five wagons; each was drawn by animals better adapted for doing the hauling than working the cattle. Since Stone would be making his home permanently at their destination, two of these—the first carrying his wife and a young woman married to one of the trail hands and serving as her maid-cum-housekeeper—had household furniture aboard. The third, known as a "blattin' cart," was used for transporting calves that were born along the way and could not as yet keep up with their mothers.

It was more usual to see the remaining pair of vehicles with a trail herd. The bed wagon, in addition to serving to transport various supplies—including, among other items, a thick rope to provide an extemporized corral into which the horses were placed for their riders to catch those selected for the day's work, a keg of ready-made horseshoes, known as "good-enoughs," as temporary replacements, and the means to fix horseshoes in place—carried the bedrolls of the crew when not in use, each man being responsible for placing his own there before starting out in the morning. If this was overlooked once, the cook would rectify the situation to the accompaniment of suitable comments on the owner's return. However, should the failure occur again, the cook was at liberty to leave it behind.

A further function of the bed wagon was to provide accommodation of a primitive nature for the nighthawk, whose purpose was to keep watch over the *remuda* through the hours of darkness. Regarded as performing a menial, albeit important task, he was expected to get what sleep he could inside during the daytime while it was keeping pace with the herd, regardless of how rough the terrain being traversed. The majority of the crew had been employed in a similar fashion earlier in their career, and although they rarely expressed the sympathy they felt over his lot, they invariably told the nighthawk that the way he had to live was all part of the process they called "making a hand." Stone considered himself fortunate on the drive to have obtained the services of a Negro who had given the name "Tarbrush," saying when asking to be taken on, that he preferred it to the one supplied by his family. He had quickly proved to be more experienced in the task than was generally the case, and, in fact, frequently stated that he was so used to doing it he could hardly stay awake during the day.

Last, but far from least, was the specially adapted vehicle that was the pride and domain of the cook. Generally an experienced old-timer, the cook ranked next below the *segundo* in order of importance and accounted himself even higher when camp was formed. Not only was he responsible for ensuring that food was available for the hands regardless of the weather conditions and hot strong coffee ready for the entire camp, he was expected to be able to attend to injuries and illness sustained by the crew.

Under the supervision of the wrangler while on the move and until the nighthawk took over, about the same distance and toward the rear on the other flank was the *remuda* of spare horses to be used when those currently being ridden became tired. Again, although the duty was essential, the work tended to be carried out by a youngster who was not considered sufficiently experienced to be riding herd on the cattle. It was the hope of every wrangler—and nighthawk too—to attain the accolade "He never lost a horse."

Almost every member of the crew had long experience and the trail was already several weeks old, so the herd had settled down to a great extent. But there was more to keeping the cattle moving than merely riding alongside them in the position assigned by the *segundo* each morning. Particularly where the longhorns were concerned—although the Herefords were far from being devoid of the trait—there were frequently attempts made to leave the line for one reason or another. When that happened the nearest of the cowhands, generally cursing such behavior with a fluency and breadth of profanity depending upon the individual's ability along those lines, would send his horse forward swiftly and direct the beast back to its companions.

Another task that Stone insisted upon being performed as a matter of precaution—and to save time later—was to

ensure that cattle occupying the range through which the
herd was traveling did not decide to join it. Accepting that
there would inevitably be a few that succeeded, he considered the extra effort required to keep these mishaps to a
minimum worth the effort. And although they might com-
plain bitterly about it as they did everything else—this being a trait of cowhands—his men understood and agreed
with his motives.

On the point of the herd, Stone and Waggles saw a big
brown and white steer that had caused trouble on previous
occasions burst from among the other cattle and dash away.
Letting out an angry exclamation, the *segundo* reached
toward the rope strapped to the low horn of his Texas-style
saddle. Before he could liberate it, he saw the nearest cowhand already in motion and, duplicating the man's action,
shook open the loop of the lariat. Realizing who the cowhand was, he felt a touch of anxiety. Oswald "Thorny"
Bush had acquired an acceptable ability at performing the
ordinary tasks, but Waggles considered the way he was
clearly contemplating dealing with the fleeing animal to be
biting off more than he could chew.

Tall and skinny, although filling out in a way that was a
tribute to the excellence of Chow Willicka's cooking, Bush
was a moderately good-looking blond youngster who
sought to appear older than his seventeen years by letting
his hair grow as profusely as it would on his top lip. His
clothing showed that he had not been shirking his work,
and around his waist was a gunbelt with a brace of white-
handled Colt Civilian Model Peacemakers in the cross-
draw holsters. Like another two of his six-horse mount, the
horse he was sitting was a paint.

Urging his horse forward and letting it build to a gallop,
the youngster closed with the fleeing steer. Arriving at a
suitable distance, he gave the rope a twirl upward and then
sent it sailing ahead so that its loop dropped in a head-

catch over the wide spread of horns that gave the breed its name. However, the running noose did not pass down to neck level. Instead, having attained the first part of his intention in a way the watching *segundo* could not fault, he just as deftly drew the slack from the loop until it tightened around the base of the bony appendages. With this achieved, he kept advancing until he had gained sufficient slack to flip the spoke of the rope—as the section between the noose and the end was called, although the word "stem" was also employed—so it fell over the animal's opposite flank and around the rump beneath the tail.

"Now comes the tricky part!" Waggles said quietly, despite his satisfaction with all he had seen so far.

"Why, sure," Stone agreed, hoping that the youngster would come to no harm as a result of adopting such a risky measure instead of just turning the animal by getting alongside and using the coiled rope as a whip.

Both of the men were willing to concede that, in addition to having brought off the first part of the throw in a competent fashion, Bush had mastered the rest of it with a similar skill. At his signal, obeying as it had been trained, the paint turned at an angle of about forty-five degrees from the steer's path. Not only did the tightened noose twist its head around and back, the spoke snatched the hind legs from the ground so that the steer reversed its direction in a violent corkscrew somersault. Landing with a resounding thud, it was so badly dazed by the impact that it was unable to resist when the youngster sprang from his saddle and darted over to remove the rope. He was back astride the horse before his victim was able to rise. Getting up on far-from-steady legs, and finding itself facing the herd, the steer trotted back to the safety of the ranks.

Responding to the whoop of approval from the next man down the line with a wave of his hand, Bush suddenly became aware that he was being watched by his boss and *segundo.* Knowing that the method he had used to deal with the situation occasionally injured or killed the steer, he was uncertain whether they would approve as well. To add to his consternation, as he was starting to draw in and coil his rope, the two men—for whom he had admiration not exceeded by that given to any other man he had ever met—rode his way.

"Good work, Thorny," Stone praised, guessing what was in the youngster's mind and wanting to put him at ease.

"You took that sucker down as pretty as I've seen it done," Waggles supplemented, always willing to give praise when it was due, and particularly when the recipient was an eager youngster who consistently showed a willingness to try to do his best.

"I hoped I wouldn't bust its fool neck," Bush admitted. "Which I've been to—allus found right easy to do."

"That it is," Stone agreed, hiding his amusement at the way the statement was amended to hide the fact that the feat had been performed for the first time. "I don't know how *you* see it, Thorny, but I figure I'd sooner have a bunch-quitter like him made wolf bait when he goes rather than give the others similar notions."

"I've allus seen it that way myself, Cap'n Hart," the youngster declared, feeling fit to burst with pride at having had his opinion requested in such a fashion. "Well, I'd best get back and see that no more of them try quitting."

"I hope they don't," Waggles commented dryly, yet without any suggestion of malice or derision, as Bush was riding back toward the cattle. "He'll bust one's neck if he keeps at it, and the kind that go are always as tough as old boot solings when Chow gets them in the cooking pot."

1. Colonel Charles Goodnight makes guest appearances in GOOD-NIGHT'S DREAM, FROM HIDE AND HORN, SET TEXAS BACK ON HER FEET, WHITE INDIANS, *and* IS-A-MAN.

2. How the riding accident befell General Jackson Baines "Ole Devil" Hardin is told in Part Three, "The Paint," THE FASTEST GUN IN TEXAS.
2b. Information regarding the career of the General is given in the Ole Devil Hardin, Civil War and Floating Outfit series; also Part Four, "Mr. Colt's Revolving Cylinder Pistol," J.T.'S HUNDREDTH. His death is reported in DOC LEROY, M.D.
3. How such factories in Texas were operated during their heyday is described in THE HIDE AND TALLOW MEN.
4. What took place during the course of one drive to a railroad town in Kansas is told in TRAIL BOSS.
5. How Captain Stone Hart received the scar is told in MISSISSIPPI RAIDER.
6. Whether raising Hereford cattle was a viable prospect under the conditions prevailing in the West was still the subject of debate at the time of the events recorded in CURE THE TEXAS FEVER.

2

A MIGHTY STRANGE WAY
TO MAKE A LIVING

"GODDAMN it to hell 'n' all ways, Dude, I *hate* cows!" declared the shorter of the two riders. They had brought their horses to a halt and allowed the pair with whom they were working to keep going in the wake of the cattle. Before he spoke, he had drawn down the bandanna he had had covering his mouth and nostrils to protect them from the dust rising behind the cattle, one of the least cared for aspects of handling a trail drive. His voice had the lazy drawl as much indicative of his being a Texan as was his dust-encrusted cowhand attire, and produced a volume of resonance that was surprising because it originated from such a small—albeit sturdy—frame. Lifting the canteen suspended from the opposite side of his double-girthed saddle's low horn to his coiled thirty-foot-long manila rope, which was of three-strand construction and laid extra hard for strength and smoothness, he removed the stopper and took a drink. Then, handing it to the man by his side, he continued in a similarly disgusted tone, "My pappy hated *cows*, which my grandpappy, his grandpappy, and his grandpappy before him, going all the way right back to Silent the Churchman, him as was altar boy for Friar Tuck in that Limey owlhoot, 'Robbing' Hood's, band, I tell you truthful true, they each 'n' every last one of 'em *all* hated cows!"

"A man'd say that's surely hating from here to there 'n' back the long ways, Silent," the second cowhand conceded dryly. He uncovered his equally tanned, albeit more handsome, features so he too could drink. His face showed more satisfaction than seemed justified, considering the lukewarm condition of the water, and he grinned at the apparently disgruntled outburst from his shorter companion. Despite the length of the drive, and although it had frequently been the subject of comment by those fortunate enough to have been privy to its delivery, this was the first time he had heard the tirade, and he found it amusing. His manner of speech and clothing, the latter showing good quality and the height of range-country fashion beneath the all-pervading coating of trail dust, indicated that he too hailed from the Lone Star State. Replacing the stopper and returning the receptacle, he went on, "Which being, there's some's'd say as how you sure picked a mighty strange way to make a living."

"Hell, Dude, I didn't mind it when Wedge wasn't doing more'n just trailing the sons of bitches north to the railroad in Kansas," Virgil "Silent" Churchman answered. He went on far from softly, and continuing to sprinkle his words with profanities in a fashion at odds with his name.[1] " 'Cause I knowed then as how they'd be took east, butchered, 'n' fed to a whole slew of goddamned *Yankees;* which same gives them said Yankees their needings for being Yankees, even though not everybody can be right fortunate enough to be born Texans. Anyways, while so doing, we didn't have to worry none about toting son-of-a-bitching *calves* along like we are now. We'd either kill 'em 'n' eat 'em all tasty in one of Chow's son-of-a-bitch stews, or give 'em to some nester to raise—said nester not knowing no better—and get rid of 'em all the sooner. Now 'n' when we get to Stone's spread, we're going to be working around the blasted critters all year long."

"Anyways, that latter's soon enough settled, *amigo*," pointed out the taller rider, who was known by no other name than the one his companion had used. However, the less-than-immaculate condition to which his clothing had been reduced by its covering of dust and stains gave little indication of how the sobriquet was acquired. "You can allus quit Wedge and find some other kind of a chore that won't take you anywheres near cows."

"Doing that'd mean *working* and, even worser, most like' doing it *afoot*!" Silent gasped in what sounded like genuine horror. "Hell's 'fire 'n' damnation, Dude, I ain't *never* done none of *that*, 'specially when it meant *walking*, since Stone had the remarkable good fortunate to have me start riding for Wedge back after the War."

"Then you've surely got yourself what some'd call a problem," the handsome cowhand admitted, eyeing his companion with what could have been taken for sympathy. "We'd best get back to helping Rusty 'n' Peaceful haze along them cows you're so all-fired fond of, else we could the both of us wind up by having to look for some other kind of work, and, like you, I *never* took kind' to working."

Despite the comments they had passed about a disinclination to doing any work, neither of the Texans mentioned the worst aspect of the task upon which they were engaged. In large part because of the dirt and dust kicked up in the dry weather, handling the drag was by far the most onerous—as well as a most important—part of handling cattle on a trail drive.

As was always the case when cattle were moved for any

distance, the rearmost section of the line comprised the footsore, the weak, the weary, and, put in human terms, the plain lazy among them. Such animals needed constant supervision and inducement to keep moving. In the most extreme and tiring form, doing this entailed grabbing hold of one that was lying down and hauling it to its feet by sheer strength. As Silent had commented, although he knew and approved of the reason because of how it could affect the future of his well-liked boss, there was a further burden for the drag riders on the present trail drive—the calves that had been born along the way and had become too large to be accommodated in the "blattin' cart." They tended to fall back to the rear, and their bawling on realizing they were no longer together would bring their mothers in search of them—to the disruption of the other members of the herd.

Because of the disadvantages and extra toil required, riding "drag" at the rear of the column was the least liked occupation for the cowhand. Unless men who had in some way aroused the dislike of the trail boss or his *segundo* were selected, it was usually given to the least competent members of the crew. However, neither contingency applied to Silent or Dude. Regardless of the layers of dust that coated both from head to foot, anybody who knew the West in general and the cattle business in particular also knew that each man was a top hand. The real reason for their presence riding the drag was that practically all the other members of the crew were of a comparable quality. Therefore, being fair dealers in all matters, Stone Hart and Waggles Harrison operated a rota system: everybody took an equal turn at the less salubrious assignment in the rear.

"Goddamn it!" Silent exclaimed after he had suspended the canteen from the saddle horn. He was about to return the folded bandanna to its position over his nose and mouth, but instead he gestured to where one of the Hereford cows which were mingled with the more numerous

Texas longhorns was swinging away from the rest to the rear of the other pair of drag riders. "Where the hell does that goddamned fool Limey critter reckon it's going?"

"Into the bushes, I'd say at a guess," Dude replied, and having drawn the appropriate conclusions before the creature went out of sight among an area of undergrowth they were passing, continued, "And them not being so modest as they do it all hid away just like us human beings when they want to go, she must've heard what you said about hating cows and reckoned being around you wasn't no place for a lady since that's what she is."

"Well, it's son-of-a-bitching going to be!" Silent asserted in tones of annoyance. "If *I've* got to put up with being 'round a bunch of goddamned cows, she can likewise. Want to go help Rusty 'n' Peaceful tend to the rest while I fetch her back?"

"Why, sure," the handsome cowhand confirmed. "I don't have nothing else better to do right now."

Replacing his bandanna, Dude set his horse moving in the direction of the other cowhands riding the drag. Having no need to take the precaution immediately, and having to answer the "call of nature," Silent allowed his own bandanna to dangle around his neck. By the time he had risen in the stirrups and relieved himself, the red and white cow had disappeared into the island-like area of fairly thick, scrubby undergrowth that spread a short distance from the line of march taken by the trail herd.

Growling the usual profanities he employed when commenting upon the stupidity of all "goddamned cows" unless there were members of the opposite sex present, past experience having taught him that doing so added to his determination to retrieve the absconding creature, Silent set his horse moving toward the bushes. Although not dense enough to impede his movements, they were of such a height that, even by once more rising in his stirrup irons, he was unable to see the animal. Nor was he able to hear sounds of its progress through the undergrowth. Scanning the ground, he found signs that told him where the Hereford had entered the bushes, but after he had followed for a short way, he was unable to locate any more indications of its passage. Keeping his mount moving, he glanced at the sky and saw the black shape of a turkey vulture starting to spiral upon widespread wings overhead. A moment later another of the birds approached and others began to converge from different directions.

Although the stocky cowhand was all too aware of the ability of the winged scavengers to find either a carcass or an animal close to death, he did not think they would help him locate his quarry. It had shown no noticeable sign of distress when quitting the herd, and he doubted it had attained such a dire condition that it had come to the attention of the birds in the brief period it was beyond his range of vision. Then a sound came to his ears and, going by past experience, he concluded it was made by one of the "cows"—by which term he designated all of the species impartially, regardless of whether he was referring to a newly born calf, yearling male, heifer, steer, or mossy-horned bull—in some kind of suffering. Knowing the terrain he was traversing was a habitat much favored by rattlesnakes, he wondered whether the errant cow had approached without being detected, blundered into one, and been bitten.

Setting his horse into motion at a steady walk, Silent approached an open area and discovered that he had achieved part of his purpose. However, the sight that met his gaze caused him to rein in his mount and prompted another profanity to leave his lips. In the center of the clearing, the cow was lying on her side with her body jerking convulsively and continuing the moaning that had first attracted his attention. On the point of resuming his ap-

proach, he remembered the supposition he had formed
regarding the possible cause of her behavior, and decided it
might be ill-advised for him to do so immediately. He wondered whether she had been struck by a rattlesnake that
had refrained from giving the usual warning, and he started
to scan the ground ahead in an attempt to locate it.

There was no sign of a rattlesnake in spite of the careful
scrutiny conducted by the cowhand, and his attention was
soon diverted to the cow. For some reason he could not
fathom, it remained lying on its left flank for a few seconds
with all four legs jerking spasmodically. Then, following a
particularly vigorous movement without any attempt made
by the cow to rise from the prone position, something that
moved and glistened as if wrapped in a kind of glossy
sheath began emerging slowly from her rear end, and he
wondered for a moment what it might be.

Despite having spent all his life in cattle country, except
for the three years when he had ridden under his present
employer's command with General Hood's Texas Brigade
during the War Between the States, Silent had never seen
the act of giving birth take place—whether by a human
being or an animal. Therefore, on realizing what was happening, he slipped from his saddle and, releasing his kettle-
bellied bay gelding—knowing that it was sufficiently well
trained to stand ground-hitched—remained where he was
to watch in a fascinated fashion that the other members of
the Wedge trail crew would have found most amusing in
view of his often-repeated declaration of a hatred of
"cows."

Suddenly, with the calf's head and forelegs having
emerged, the cow lurched to her feet. Much to his concern,
Silent watched the still-covered and feebly moving shape
slide from inside its mother's back passage at an increased
pace. It thudded to the ground behind her and, after a few
seconds of weak struggling, gave vent to what—although he

could not have expressed the sensation in words—he regarded as being a blatt filled with pathos. However, it apparently suffered no ill effects from what the watching cowhand had considered a most callous act on the part of its mother.

What the cowhand did not know until it was explained to him later by somebody better informed on the subject was that he had just witnessed nature's equivalent of a human doctor slapping the rump of a newborn baby to set its lungs working by bringing forth a yell. The calf let out a surprisingly loud bawl and wriggled with an increased vigor that caused the embryonic sac to split; aided by its mother's licking at it, further struggles drew the sac even more clear.

Like many men who profess to have a hard-boiled nature, Silent had a soft spot where children and very young animals were concerned. This tender feeling extended, of course, to the calf he had just seen enter the world and which he viewed with considerable curiosity and favor. Indeed, he regarded it with what came close to being an avuncular interest. And as he watched its struggles while trying to stand, he considered the seeming indifference of its mother as no more than could be expected from one of her sex and kind.

"Well, do *something*, you useless hunk of walking beef fit only for some blasted Yankee to eat!" the cowhand growled. "Goddamn it, that's *your* kid down there needing help, and he's sure as sin's for sale in Cowtown not getting none from you!"

Not unexpectedly, the new mother paid no attention to the indignant words. Nor, much to Silent's continued annoyance, did she make any attempt to assist the calf when, still wet from the sac out of which it had liberated itself, the calf finally made its feet. Wobbling on uncertain legs and almost going down a couple of times, with the admiring cowhand urging it on verbally and mentally, it found its way to its mother's udder. Once there, closing its mouth on a teat and filled with enthusiasm over having located the source of a well-deserved meal, it started to suckle with a vigor that earned the watching man's approbation.

"Looks like you're all right now, li'l buddy," Silent commented, but he directed a baleful scowl at the cow. "Not that it's any of *your* doing, you slab-sided apology for a mother. The li'l 'n' done it all on his lonesome."

Even as he was speaking, he was attracted by a rustling sound from the bushes at the side opposite to where he had arrived in the clearing, and swung his face in that direction. What he saw brought a low rumble of concern and anger from him.

1. See paragraph four of our Author's Note.

3

I WOULDN'T HAVE BROUGHT
MARGARET ALONG

"For all I've known his pappy a fair few years, I wasn't overkeen on having him along when he asked to come along on the drive," Stone Hart remarked, watching until Thorny Bush resumed the routine work interrupted by chasing the steer. Then, starting to turn and set his *bayos-cebrunos* gelding at a walk in the direction the herd was traveling, he continued, "But, despite the way he's got himself armed and dotes on riding paints, he's doing all right."

"I don't reckon Cap'n Fog'd take kind to hearing that 'despite'," Waggles Harrison drawled, aware of in whose honor the youngster had selected his armament and preference in color for the horses selected to be his mount. "But I go along with you. He's no show-off, nor trigger fast 'n' up-from-Texas kid allus on the prod for any excuse to start using them fancy white-handled Colt guns. Fact being, he never tries to prove he can use 'em, even though he can passably. Top of that, 'cepting he was just a smidgen too eager to make good first off, way he's never pulled back from *any* chore he's been handed, I reckon he's making a hand."

"You won't get any argument from me on that," Stone declared, knowing Bush would have been delighted with thelast part of his *segundo*'s comment. It implied that the youngster had not been found wanting in any aspect of his duties or way of living among older men with more experience. "I just hope he doesn't go the same way as that kid who was wrangler for Dusty when he took the Rocking H herd to Dodge against Wyatt Earp's saying it wasn't to come."

"Do you reckon anything like that could happen to him where we're going?" Waggles inquired somberly, knowing the fate that had befallen Little Jackie the wrangler on the trail drive in question.[1]

"I've got no reason to think it should," Stone admitted, but something in the way he was speaking drew his companion's eyes his way. "Did I have, I wouldn't have brought Margaret along, or let her come until I was sure everything was going to be all right."

"I'd have admired to see you try stopping her," the *segundo* claimed, a grin coming to his leathery face. "The boss lady's one to stand aside from when she gets bound and determined to do something."

"She's all of that and more, *amigo*," the trail boss affirmed, and glanced to where his wife was sitting on the box of the leading wagon, giving no indication of her physical disability.

"Know something, boss?" Waggles asked, having gotten out of the habit of remembering that Margaret Hart was blind. "I've a feeling you haven't been quite as easy as you might about coming out to take over your uncle's spread."

"Well, there're things about the way it came to me that I'm a mite curious over," Stone conceded, aware that their long association had enabled Waggles to read his moods even though the puzzlement he had experienced had not previously been discussed between them. "Uncle Cornelius Maclaine was never close even to Momma. Fact being, we'd never heard a word from him after she got married on account of Pappy wasn't a Yankee. So the last thing I'd have expected was for him to leave me his spread in his will."

"Could be he had a change of heart," the *segundo* suggested. "I've heard tell as sometimes folks do, even though they be Yankees. Or didn't have no other kin, leastwise any he liked well enough to want to pass it on to."

"I wouldn't know about that," Stone said with a wry grin. "But Momma always used to reckon he wouldn't change his winter long johns and socks come summer until folks started backing off downwind from him."

Despite the lighthearted way in which the trail boss was speaking, he was correct about the feelings the unexpected bequest of the ranch had engendered. In fact, he had forgotten about the existence of his maternal uncle until, on his return from his latest trail drive, a member of the Pinkerton National Detective Agency acting on behalf of Cornelius Maclaine had brought him the news that he had inherited a ranch in Arizona. Finding Stone had not required any great powers of deduction, nor the employment of that already famous—if not always liked, on account of questionable methods it was alleged to use on behalf of its clients—organization's excellent facilities for picking up information. It was well known that he based himself in San Antonio de Bexar between drives and could be contacted by leaving a message at the bar of the Bull's Head Saloon, the owner of which was a friend of long standing.

When questioned by Stone, the meeting having taken place in person, the operative could give little information about the spread other than its location. However, he had stated that he had been asked to say there were no out-

standing debts to be settled. What was more, not only were
the taxes levied by the authorities in what was still a territory and not a state of the Union covered until the end of
the year, but the same applied to the wages—paid by Counselor Edward Sutherland, the lawyer in Child City, seat of
Spanish Grant County, who handled the affair—of the men
hired to take care of the property until he arrived to assume control.

The news had come at a time when Stone was facing a
dilemma.

When it had become obvious that war could not be
avoided, Stone had decided like many others being trained
as potential officers in the United States Military Academy
at West Point on the Hudson River in southeast New York
State, that his support must be given to the Southern cause.
Like the majority of Texans who shared the sentiment, he
had not been led to the conclusion by a desire to retain
ownership of slaves; like many others in Texas, his family
had never owned any, or wished to. Rather, he was impelled by the knowledge that, under the Constitution, any
state finding its policies incompatible with those the federal
government was trying to impose had the right to secede
from the Union. Therefore, he had taken the privilege offered by the Commanding Officer of the Academy to all
who shared his point of view and resigned.

Although Stone had never acquired the well-deserved
fame of Turner Ashby, John Singleton "the Gray Ghost"
Mosby, and the Lone Star State's own Dusty Fog as a cavalry leader, nor specialized as they had in carrying out raiding expeditions that caused the Yankees grave problems, he
had served with distinction. On recuperating from the
wound gained when he saved the life of Belle Boyd, he had
been assigned to help Colonel Jubal Early deliver herds of
longhorn cattle required to feed General Ole Devil Hardin's Army of Arkansas and North Texas in its fight to hold

on to the first state.[2] The experience he had gained in the performance of that important—albeit less-than-glamorous—duty was to serve him in good stead when, accepting that the military career for which he had been trained was no longer possible, he went back to civilian life.

Returning to Texas, Stone had found his prospects far from rosy. His parents had died in his absence and, flocking like vultures to feed on a corpse, Yankee carpetbaggers—with the support of the State Police, who had replaced the Texas Rangers with the authority of the federal government's Reconstruction Administration led by Governor Bartholomew Davis—made the most of their opportunities to turn a profit in every way possible. The Hart ranch was only one to fall into such grasping hands under the excuse of payment of the requisite taxes having lapsed.[3]

Faced by the need to find gainful employment, like many other returning veterans who had supported the South, Stone had turned to the cattle business. When the trail drives had begun, he had seen a way by which he could turn the knowledge acquired under Jubal Early to his advantage. Instead of going to work for one of the large spreads that sent their own cattle, he had elected to offer his services to those ranchers who had less stock and could not afford the expense of sending the comparatively small amounts available to the lucrative markets available only in far-off Kansas. Gathering the nucleus of what became known as the Wedge crew—the road brand he adopted, to establish his right to deliver the cattle bearing the indications of ownership by his clients, was shaped like such a tool—he had commenced operations.

Such was the success Stone and the Wedge crew achieved that they had continued to be engaged in the lucrative occupation for several years. One unusual assignment to come their way was driving a herd of buffalo—a species already badly depleted by hunting for hides and meat—to a place set out as a sanctuary.[4] However, the time had come when the curtailment of their source of income was a real possibility.

Prior to leaving on the latest-completed trail drive, Stone had met and married the daughter of one of the ranchers for whom he was taking cattle to the railroad shipping point in Kansas. Because of the scar left by the saber of the Yankee he had prevented from killing the Rebel Spy, he had previously tended to shy away from the company of what were classed as "good" women by the standards of the day; he believed that the disfigurement of his features the scar caused would be regarded with revulsion by them. Nor had he ever considered forming any permanent attachment to the occasional female companions he met in saloons.

From the beginning of their acquaintance, Margaret Goddard had never struck him in such a fashion. Nor had this been entirely due to her having lost her eyesight in a childhood accident. In fact, such was her capability at coping with most things around the ranch house that had always been her home that he had not realized she was blind until he saw her walking outside with Rolf, the dog that served a vital purpose in helping her overcome her disability. One of the chocolate-colored retrievers originally bred for the demanding task of collecting waterfowl killed by hunters from the icy cold and often rough water of Chesapeake Bay, it possessed, despite being large and powerful, an intelligence and tractable nature that allowed it to take to the tasks of what in a later period would be termed a seeing-eye dog.

There had been factors causing Stone to think about making a change to his way of life even before he had learned of the bequest from his uncle. For one thing, such had been the number of animals sent to Kansas that many of the owners who used his services were having difficulty keeping the level of their remaining stock at a viable level.

Consequently, they were either selling out to larger ranchers or holding on to the remaining animals so as to let the herds increase. Another factor was the way in which railroads were beginning to be constructed: many branch lines connected to the main intercontinental route in Kansas. Although they had not yet removed the need for Texans to make the long drive north, eventually they would bring an end to the need for the Wedge crew's specialized occupation. Lastly, and by far the most important consideration where Stone was concerned, was that although Margaret had made no complaint, he had no desire to leave her behind for the lengthy periods he would be absent on the trail.

Having saved a considerable portion of his earnings against such an eventuality, Stone had the means to purchase a small ranch. Margaret had an older brother who was a competent hand in all aspects of running their property and had, in fact, been on a trail drive with Wedge. Stone—with her agreement—had declined an offer from her father to make his home there instead of buying some other property. However, the arrival of the Pinkerton agent had prevented his having to do either. Having no information about the state of the stock at the ranch in Arizona, he had decided to make sure that there was the nucleus of a breeding herd by taking some of his own along. Showing none of the conservatism of some ranchers where the possibility of raising Hereford cattle on a comparatively free-ranging basis was concerned, he had elected to invest some of his capital in purchasing enough bulls and cows to become established in their new home.

Although a couple of his regular Wedge hands were unavailable due to private affairs demanding their attention, Stone experienced no difficulty in gathering the crew required to move the cattle from Texas to Arizona. Waggles Harrison and the remaining regulars immediately offered their services after being informed of what was contemplated. Stating that he did not consider it fair for other members of his honored occupation to be saddled with cooking for such a worthless and unappreciative bunch, Chow Willicka—if anybody had ever discovered his given name, it was not disclosed—announced that he would, out of the goodness of his heart.

Aided by Tarbrush, who arrived one morning and said he had heard somebody was needed as nighthawk and that he had urgent reasons for wishing to avoid being found by an unspecified number of outraged fathers of ladies of his acquaintance, Arnold Watts—claiming to have become infected by Silent Churchman's frequently stated hatred of "cows"—was eager to retain his position as wrangler for the *remuda* despite being qualified to ride the herd. Drawn by the mysterious "prairie telegraph" that could spread news at surprising speed across the range, enough men of the quality Stone required had soon arrived. He had yielded, not without reluctance, to the request from an old friend to take Thorny Bush along. However, despite the youngster's lack of experience, he had so far been given no cause to regret the decision.

Two potential difficulties had been solved to Stone's complete satisfaction.

Jonathan Ambrose Raybold—who had frequently taken grave exception to being addressed by either Christian name instead of Johnny—had been compelled to go to New York on urgent family business,[5] and was unavailable to perform the very important function of scout. However, a most adequate replacement had been found through the auspices of Ole Devil Hardin. The misgivings Stone had experienced over taking Margaret away from the familiar surroundings in which she had grown up were lessened to a great extent by another development. It was Jason Willis who provided a suitable solution.

Since they were sidekicks from childhood days in Texas, Rusty—as he insisted upon being called—would have gone with Doc Leroy to help follow up a tip that it was hoped would lead to the hired gunfighter Hayden Paul Lindrick, whom they blamed for the murder of Doc's parents.[6] However, Rusty had sustained a fall while taking the bedsprings out of the belly of a newly acquired addition to the Wedge's *remuda*. The injury was serious enough for him to be confined to a sickbed under the care of an attractive and most efficient nurse. The bond that developed between them had proved so strong that, claiming what was good enough for Stone, Dusty Fog, and Red Blaze was good enough for him,[7] he had proposed marriage and been accepted. As a result, Stephanie Willis had not only agreed to accompany her husband to Arizona, where he would remain as a member of the Wedge, she had volunteered to take on the duties of maid and housekeeper until Margaret was used to coping with the new environment at the ranch. The proposition had been gratefully accepted and, each possessing an adaptable and amiable personality, the two young women quickly became good friends.

The drive from Texas had so far been accomplished with only a few problems, and none of a serious nature. Stone had often blessed his good fortune in having such a competent crew. Under the supervision of Waggles, whose duties as *segundo* brought him closer than the trail boss to the crew, the newcomers had formed into a smoothly functioning team. Nor had there been any friction between them and the old hands. Having been born and raised among cowhands, Bush had accepted that he must stand for some ribbing on account of his youth. He soon began to counter it with assertions that he was surrounded by a bunch of old and decrepit men who ought by rights to be hard-wintering around the stove in the bunkhouse instead of trying to act as if they were still prime, hale, and hearty.

Nor was there ever any objectionable treatment accorded to Tarbrush because of his race and color. Realizing the importance of his work, even without needing to be told to do so, the crew did all they could to minimize the noise they made near the bed wagon while he was sleeping. In fact, the only piece of trouble involving Tarbrush took place at a saloon in New Mexico when a drunken mule-skinner who claimed to have fought in the Union Army during the War Between the States referred to him as a "goddamned uppity nigger." During the course of the ensuing conflict, the offending man and the barroom sustained considerable damage at the hands of the outraged Texans. However, the owner—also a Southron—had informed the local peace officers that the injured man had caused the fuss and attached no blame for the fracas to his fellow Johnny Rebs, so they were allowed to go on their way after paying a nominal fine.

"I've got kin like tha—!" Waggles began, amused by the less-than-flattering assessment of her uncle made by the now-deceased Mrs. Hart. Then he swung his gaze ahead and went on in what Stone realized was a subtly different tone, "Looks like we've got us some company coming, and I can't say I'm taken with the look of them."

1. What happened to the wrangler, Little Jackie, is told in TRAIL BOSS.
2. Information about the activities of the Confederate States Army of Arkansas and North Texas is given in the Civil War series.
3. How the life of another Texan, John Wesley Hardin, was ruined by the excesses of the Reconstruction period is told in THE HOODED RIDERS.
4. Told in BUFFALO ARE COMING.
5. What happened as a result of Johnny Raybold's trip to New York is told in THE RIO HONDO WAR and GUNSMOKE THUNDER.
6. How Marvin Eldridge "Doc" Leroy's hunt for Hayden Paul Lindrick progressed and he attained his ambition to become a qualified medical practitioner, as his father was before him, is told in DOC LEROY, M.D.
7. What led up to the marriages of Dusty Fog and Red Blaze is told in DECISION FOR DUSTY FOG and WAGONS TO BACKSIGHT, respectively.

4

THAT'S *ALL* I GODDAMNED NEED!

Walking with the soles of all four feet placed flat on the ground in the manner known as plantigrade, the black bear, whose faint noises made while approaching through the bushes had attracted the attention of Silent Churchman, came to a halt on reaching the edge of the clearing, as if surprised to find other living creatures there. However, the stocky cowhand felt sure that could not be the case. In fact, he could guess what had brought it there at such an inopportune moment. It had been attracted by a combination of the sound made by the cow in what he later discovered were called her labor pains and possibly the scent caused by the birth. Whatever the reason might be, Silent was far from pleased by the sight of the bear.

Going by what happened next, the red and white Hereford cow and Silent's kettle-bellied bay horse were thinking along the same lines. Each decided that being in close proximity to such a large and potentially dangerous wild animal was a situation not to be endured. Therefore, each took immediate measures to remove itself from the locality. Paying not the slightest attention to the tiny morsel of life it had so recently brought into the world, apart from snatching free the teat of the udder being sucked, the cow spun and fled away from the threat, proceeding in the direction from which it had come. Although of phlegmatic temperament under normal conditions, the horse was just as swift in its reactions. Letting out a snort of alarm, it twirled with the agility that was used to good advantage in the performance of its work, and, more by accident than intent, lit out ahead of the cow.

Under different circumstances, for all his often-expressed sentiments about a lack of intelligence being a quality of "cows," Silent might have conceded—albeit in a grudging fashion—that there was some excuse for the way in which the mother of the newly born calf responded. Unlike the Texas longhorns, whose progenitors had long enough experience at free-ranging and fending for themselves to teach habits that helped keep their young from danger, the Hereford strain was not all that long ago brought to the United States from a country where, he had been informed, the largest predatory creature likely to be met was a red fox or badger. A longhorn cow, even having been through its first pregnancy, finding itself in a similar position would have charged without hesitation in defense of its newly born offspring. However, lacking any such maternal instinct, or having it overridden by its fear of the unknown, the Hereford abandoned the calf to save itself. Finding itself deprived of the warm milk it had been extracting, the little creature let out a protesting bawl. Then it attempted to go after its hurriedly departing mother, but its legs were incapable of such an effort and it toppled to the ground. Starting to struggle erect, it continued to let loose its high-pitched vocal protests.

There was, the cowhand told himself bitterly and pro-

fanely under his breath, only himself to blame for the way
in which his normally reliable horse behaved. While waiting
for the drive to Arizona to begin, he had eagerly taken an
opportunity to indulge in a favorite pastime by going out
with a pack of big-game hounds after a stock-killing male
black bear.[1] After a long chase, the predator had been
brought to bay in a clearing among some fairly wide-spaced
bushes too weak to allow it to climb above the rapidly
approaching hounds. Accepting the fact, it had started to
defend itself with all the savage fury its kind were famous
for employing under similar conditions.

The lightest of the men following the hunt and seated on
the bay, which was a running fool, Silent had been the first
to arrive at the scene of the conflict. The bear gave Silent
no chance to arm himself with his Spencer No. 56 Repeating carbine, or even draw either of the holstered Colt 1860
Army revolvers that he was then wearing as defensive
weapons for use mainly one at a time at close quarters—
although, aware of his and their limitations under the prevailing conditions, he had no desire to attempt anything
with the latter unless driven to it by unavoidable circumstances. The enraged bear let out an awesome blood-
curdling bawl almost human in timbre, and while doing so,
rushed through the pack; experienced in such work, the
hounds scattered from its path.

Probably hoping to curtail the hunting of bears, the more
rabid professional conservationists of a later age would try
to claim that the species *Euarctos americanus americanus* is
a totally inoffensive creature so close to being vegetarian in
its eating habits that it hardly qualified as omnivorous. To
give strength to the argument, some even quoted the old
Indian legend that a brave who killed a black bear—but not
the larger and vastly more dangerous grizzly—was required
to apologize to its spirit for having been compelled to do
so.[2]

Although willing to concede that there was less risk involved in tangling with a black bear than with another member of the bear family, Silent had never subscribed to such an ill-advised and potentially dangerous line of thought. He hailed from a part of cattle-raising Texas noted for the prolificacy of species. Therefore, he had had sufficient dealings with those with a taste for the meat of cattle to know that they were never to be taken lightly—and even less when brought to bay by hounds set on their trail.

Even for one who had engaged in similar hunts many times, there was something awe-inspiring about the sight of a charging black bear as it approached a speed of perhaps thirty miles per hour. Its body was made to seem even more massive by the long guard hairs of its pelt, which now stood erect. Thrust ahead to the extent of its neck, the slavering jaws of its sharply pointed head—seemingly small in comparison with its bulk elsewhere—were open to show large, obviously sharp canine teeth ready to sink deeply into flesh.

The entire effect presented by the hostile bear had not been one to inspire a state of confidence on the part of the object of its hostility. Nor had Silent's generally well-behaved and steady bay considered it in such a light. Giving vent to its feelings in no uncertain fashion, it had turned with the intention of getting away to any location clear of its proposed assailant. The bay spun with an agility acquired from dodging the only slightly less dangerous charges launched by longhorn cattle. Only being a rider of exceptional skill, well-versed in remaining afork his mount in unexpected circumstances, had allowed the cowhand to avoid being flung clear.

Engrossed solely in staying in the saddle, Silent had been unable to take any kind of defensive action against the bear. Fortunately, the bay had had sufficient reaction speed to carry them clear. However, the margin of the evasion was so narrow that the bear, striking in passing without its speed diminishing to any noticeable degree, had contrived to rip a narrow scratch in the horse's rump. Taken with the fear inspired by the charge, and the pain of the slight injury, the spirited bay set off in a series of bucks that might have gladdened the hearts of spectators at a rodeo.

The cowhand had been too fully occupied by the urgent priority of remaining astraddle the horse to do more than hang tight. Fortunately, the pack of hounds were up to the occasion. Although they had very wisely allowed their quarry to pass unimpeded, they had resumed the chase as soon as the bear had gone by. Feeling itself once more being harried by the closely pressing creatures, the bear had concluded discretion to be the better part of valor and, having removed what it had regarded as another threat to its well-being, continued to race away as fast as it could move. Nor, regardless of his early eagerness to take the bear as a trophy before the rest of the party could arrive, was Silent sorry to see it go.

Although the scratch from the bear's paw had quickly healed, the bay had never forgotten how it was inflicted or what kind of dangerous beast was responsible for it. Therefore, even though the threat was not in evidence on this occasion, the horse was disinclined to remain long enough to let any such aggressive action commence. Instead, duplicating fright displayed by the Hereford cow, it forgot its training to remain motionless when its open-ended reins were dangling from its bridle and took off in the direction of the other animal.

Already fuming over the desertion of the calf by its mother, Silent was diverted from the thought of how this strengthened his hatred of "goddamned cows" by the sight of his horse following suit. He realized that this posed a very serious added threat to the existence of the calf in whose struggle for survival he had been taking such an interest. What was more, he realized that his own life might also be in danger. When hard-wintering in his later years he would attribute to it a bulk far exceeding that of even a full-grown grizzly, but in truth the bear did not come anywhere close to the size of those he had contended against and beaten in the Lone Star State. At that moment, however, he was all too aware of its close to three-hundred-pound bulk and obvious proclivity toward eating meat that made it a most dangerous adversary.

"That's *all* I goddamned need!" Silent growled bitterly, giving a brief glance after the departing bay and realizing the extremely perilous nature of the situation in which he had been placed.

Experienced in such matters and endowed with an outlook that shied against accepting such a way out, the cowhand immediately cast aside the thought of taking flight before an attack by the bear could be launched. He knew the basic trait of every carnivore impelled it to chase anything that fled from it, and he was equally aware that no man on foot—especially one wearing the high-heeled boots found necessary for their work by cowhands—could outpace a black bear should he instinctively be sought as food. To add to the dilemma, there was the safety of the newly born calf to be taken into consideration. For all that he generally professed hatred of "goddamned cows," he had already formed a liking for the little beast, and his whole being revolted against leaving it to what he knew was almost certain to be its doom. However, there were serious difficulties to be overcome in his present position before he could even try to make a change for the better.

The horse had taken off with Silent's Spencer carbine, which, despite having been acquired as a battlefield capture during the War Between the States, possessed the potency, given by its .56-caliber bullets and the seven-shot capacity of its magazine, to bring a sufficiently swift end to any aggressive action—even though he would need to operate

the lever and charge the chamber, then manually cock the
hammer. What was more, since they had been carried only
to enable the employment of twelve shots without the need
for the lengthy process of reloading with even paper car-
tridges and percussion caps after six had been discharged
from a single weapon, he did not have the benefit of the
revolvers anymore. Deciding that the time had come to
make a change in his defensive armament, he had taken
advantage of the greater rapidity with which the Colt
Peacemaker could receive its full complement of center-
fire metallic rounds to reduce the burden by carrying only
one. Although satisfied with its potency at making a stopping hit at close range, which was its purpose, he knew this
could only be achieved provided the bullet was planted in
an appropriate location.

Every instinct Silent possessed gave warning that attain-
ing the end he desired was far from guaranteed.

Growling in a menacing fashion over what it regarded as
a threat to obtaining the meal of meat it had come to
collect, the bear stood shaking its head from side to side in
a way Silent recognized as being the prelude to some form
of offensive action. Silent also realized that the bear's posture lessened the chances of his being able to make the
kind of shot he knew would be necessary. With only a
twenty-eight-grain load of black powder per bullet, the Colt
lacked at this range the kind of stopping power that would
be required to halt the big animal in its tracks. A head shot
would do, but this could only be relied upon if the bullet
entered from the side of the skull.

The cowhand had once seen a bear struck between the
eyes by a bullet from a Winchester Model of 1866 rifle.
What happened next had given added support to his often-
declared belief that such a weapon and its load, no larger
than that used for the Colt Peacemaker revolver, were puny
in comparison with his old Spencer. Even though the bullet

made contact between the eyes, there was a sufficiently
sturdy protective shield to deflect it just under the skin and
force it to pass on out. The glancing impact had been hard
enough to send the bear down like a pole-axed steer, but it
had recovered sufficiently to rise and charge the man who
had fired the shot. If it had not been for the speed with
which Silent and other members of the hunting party
opened fire from various points, the bear's attack would
have proved successful.

Bearing that experience in mind, the cowhand decided
that to shoot under the prevailing state of affairs would in
all probability do more harm than good.

Nor was Silent any more enamored of the only solution
that came to mind based on his knowledge of predatory
animals. But he was determined to try it.

"Oh well," the cowhand breathed, drawing and cocking
his Colt. "Billy Jack allus allowed how Cap'n Fog said the
best form of defense is making a head-on and horns-a-
hooking attack. I just hope that lean and miserable-looking
ole calamity-wailing cuss wasn't getting it wrong like he
most allus does."

Silent let out the loudest whoop his stocky frame was
capable of producing and charged across the clearing
toward the bear. While doing so, he fired the Colt in the
bear's general direction as fast as he could operate the
single-action mechanism, making sure he did not send
the bullets into the animal. The action might have struck an
onlooker unversed in such matters as totally reckless, but
he knew that there was a sound method in what he was
doing. Everything now hung upon whether his knowledge
of predatory creatures was correct.

For a moment, the way in which the cowhand behaved
did not evoke any response from the bear. However, like
every carnivore, it possessed a very well-developed strain of
caution in its makeup. While its size made it master of the

range over which it had gained dominance—smaller members of its species and even the occasional cougar met in its travels yielded to its superior weight and power—seeing what seemed to be a direct challenge from the strange creature it had found, apparently prepared to dispute its right to the meal it was seeking, caused it to review the situation.

If the bear had been goaded by pangs of extreme hunger, it would in all probability have acted in a different fashion. However, it was reasonably well fed and had evidently come on hearing the moan of what it sensed to be an animal in difficulty and, therefore, offering the opportunity to indulge its well-developed liking for fresh meat. Nevertheless, had the strange erect moving creature—its habits not yet having brought it into contact with men in spite of its having developed a fondness for their livestock—shown signs of backing away, it would have advanced to establish its right to the prey.

Faced by what was clearly a determined charge, to the accompaniment of thunderous crashes and spurts of flame beyond anything in its comprehension, the bear held its ground for only a few seconds. Then, as Silent's instinctive counting warned that he was firing his fifth shot—he intended to retain the remaining bullet in the cylinder as a last-minute defense should his ploy fail—the bear's instincts produced the effect he desired. The bear gave a snort and turned to dash away through the bushes.

"Whooee!" Silent exclaimed, coming to a halt and starting to reload the Colt by taking bullets from the loops on his gunbelt—one of the factors that had caused him to make the change in his defensive armament—without the need for conscious thought. "Virgil Churchman, if you want for us to grow all old 'n' ornerier than we are now, don't you *never* let me pull a fool trick like *that* again."

With that heartfelt, if basically impracticable, comment

having been delivered and his weapon made ready for immediate use if the need arose, the cowhand turned and looked over to the calf. Gazing about in what Silent regarded as a bewildered fashion, it was giving notice of its objection to being deserted by its mother. Silent already having developed a liking for what he considered to be its spunky qualities, knew it was still up to him to help it overcome the uncaring treatment it had been accorded by its mother. The solution to how this might be brought about was soon forthcoming.

By chance, Dude had been looking behind when first the Hereford cow and then Silent's bay emerged from the bushes. At any time on the open range, the sight of a riderless horse was a cause for grave concern. Therefore, the handsome cowhand had signaled for Peaceful Gunn to drop back to fill his position in the rear of the drag. No more than a quick "Silent's afoot" was needed to explain why he made the request. Catching the reins of the bay while noticing with relief that there were no indications of its rider having sustained an injury causing its loss, he had wasted no time in setting out to investigate. The sound of the yell, which he knew could only have been emitted from a set of human lungs, followed by the four shots, guided him in the proper direction.

"What's up, Silent," Dude inquired, seeking to conceal his relief at finding that his companion did not appear to be in any kind of difficulty, "get off to pick up your woolsey?"

"The hell I did," Silent yelled, oozing indignation over the suggestion that a man of his caliber would have purchased, much less be wearing, a cheap and notoriously inferior-quality "woolsey" hat even in an emergency. Doing so was the mark of a greenhorn or Westerner who lacked the qualities deemed necessary to become a top hand in the cattle business. As was always the case, his own headdress was a genuine John B. Stetson. "That goddamned cow had her a calf and run out on it."

"You sure used up a whole slew of shells trying to coax her to come back," Dude claimed, although he realized that something of far greater importance had been responsible for the firing of so many shots.

"They wasn't for *her,* you dad-blasted knobhead!" Silent yelled. He needed relief for his still-churned-up emotions, and he knew he and the other cowhand were on a footing that allowed him to use the term for an exceptionally balky and stupid mule. "Was a whole slew of the biggest goddamned black bears I've ever seen outside of Texas figuring on eating that spunky little feller, and I concluded they'd have to be stopped doing it."

"A whole slew of 'em, huh?" Dude challenged with a grin, aware that black bears never traveled in a pack, unless it was a sow with her latest batch of cubs.

"Thought I saw maybe a dozen grizzlies and a cougar or two siding 'em, but I didn't wait to take no head count," Silent asserted. "Anyways, they've all tooken a greaser standoff and won't be back. So now we've got to figure out what to do for the best with this little jasper."

"I bet Chow could use him to whomp up a dandy son-of-a-bitch stew," the handsome cowhand suggested with the air of one making an obviously provocative statement.

"Anybody even *thinks* of trying that'll right smart have to answer to *me!*" Silent declared with vehemence, acting as if he believed the proposal had been made in earnest. "Nope, he's headed for the blattin' cart and, if his momma won't own him, Rosita 'n' Mig'll feed him until he can start eating grass."

While speaking, the stocky cowhand took a couple of pigging thongs from the pocket of his Levi's. Behaving in a far more gentle way than would normally have been the case, he secured the hind legs and forelegs of the calf. With this done, he asked Dude to lend a hand in loading it onto his horse. He used his bandanna to blindfold his horse, and thus lessen the chance of the dun objecting to the unusual burden.

"Yes sir, you old cuss," Dude said, too quietly for his companion to hear, as he watched the care being taken to mount the horse and hold the little animal in position. "You surely do *hate* goddamned cows."

1. *A description of how predatory animals can be hunted by a pack of big game hounds, and some of the breeds most commonly used, is given in* HOUND DOG MAN.
2. *An example of how the Indian ritual was carried out is given in* COMANCHE.

5

MAYBE YOU'D LIKE TO CUT
THEIR THROATS

"What do you make of them, *amigo*?" Stone Hart asked, studying with range-wise eyes the half a dozen men not too far ahead who had emerged from a clump of bushes even more extensive than the one into which—although he was unaware of it, since the distance and noises from the trail herd had prevented him from hearing any of the commotion—Silent Churchman had just completed dealing with the black bear.

"Just about the same as you, boss," Waggles Harrison replied, also conducting a knowledgeable scrutiny. "I've a notion *what* they are and don't like any part of it. Don't tell me they're figuring to pull the old head-tax toll game on us. I figure that plumb went out of fashion after ole Shangai Pierce and then Cap'n Fog rode ragged over Kliddoe's bunch up to Kansas."

"Could be times are hard down to Arizona and this bunch are figuring to revive said good ole Yankee custom," Stone drawled. "Give Chow a wig-wag so he'll know what wants doing, just in case we're right about not taking to them."

"She's done," the *segundo* claimed as he twisted on his saddle and made a waving motion with his right hand. The gesture was seen and acted upon by the cook for the Wedge in the chuck wagon, for it and the others came to a halt.

Although five of the well-armed group coming toward Stone and Waggles wore attire suggesting that they could be cowhands to eyes less accustomed to such matters, neither of them assumed that to be the case. In their opinion, the quintet were the kind who—while far from being top-grade stock—took pay only for a willingness to use the guns they were wearing or carrying. Nor was the exception any different from the point of view shared by the two range-wise Texans.

Of no more than medium height, but with a chunky frame resplendent in the garb frequently adopted by professional gamblers to emphasize their affluence and draw in opponents eager to acquire some of it, the sixth man had what appeared by the shortness of their barrels to be two white-handled Colt Storekeeper Model Peacemaker revolvers with butts pointing forward in high-riding holsters on his waist belt. Beneath a low-crowned and broad-brimmed tan-colored J. B. Stetson decorated with silver conchas, his trimly mustached and not bad-looking face had less tan than the majority of cowhands had, and lines suggestive of real cruelty. He was, Stone and Waggles assessed, the acknowledged and accepted leader of the party.

"Howdy, you-all," the trail boss greeted in a neutral tone as the party came to a halt in a loose half-circle that blocked his and his *segundo*'s passage and compelled them to stop.

"You running this drive?" asked the man in the attire of a gambler, his voice gentle yet subtly menacing, and revealing an accent indicative of one born in Illinois.

"You might say that," Stone admitted, noticing the menacing way in which the rest of the group either nursed rifles or sat with hands resting on the butts of revolvers.

"Fact being," the leather-faced *segundo* drawled, lounging apparently at ease on his double-girthed Texas range saddle and deciding that none of the men before him were drawing any conclusions if they had noticed that the wagons were now halted as the herd continued its steady approach. "You just did."

"This is Circle AW range you're crossing, and has been for the past two days," the spokesman for the party announced. "Which our boss, Wilson Eardle, concludes some of his stock might have got mixed in with yours."

"Would that be accidental or purpose-done?" Waggles inquired with what appeared to be mildness.

"One way or the other makes no never mind to the boss," the gambler-dressed man replied. "He's told me what to do whenever I come across a herd."

"You being?" Stone queried.

"Name's Jeremy Korbin," the spokesman announced, his manner implying that he did not consider any further explanation necessary.

"Can't say I bring it to mind," the trail boss drawled as if regarding the matter as being of no especial importance. "How's about you, *amigo*?"

"Seems I recollect hearing of a tinhorn called it," Waggles answered, sounding just as relaxed and indifferent while holding himself at instant readiness. "Only, I don't reckon *he'd* be doing the talking for a rancher."

"These beefheads talk all big 'n' sassy, don't they, Jer?" commented a tall and lanky man whose clothing was less than clean and who rested a Spencer rifle across his knees. His voice was indicative of origins in Missouri, one of the Northern "Free" as opposed to Southern "Slave" states prior to the Civil War, which could account for the way in which he continued speaking. "Even if I couldn't afore, feeling the same way myself, I can see now why Eard—*the boss* don't cotton none to goddamned Johnny Rebs, 'specially when they hail from Texas."

"Well, I'm doing it," Korbin stated, paying no more attention to the remark just passed than he had to the reference to a "tinhorn" having his name, although the term was insulting in its implications. "Which being, we're going to cut your herd."

The declaration made, although there was no discernible change in the appearance of the speaker, the rest of his party visibly tensed.

Nothing was more likely to provoke trouble, in all probability involving gunplay, than a demand to cut another man's herd when made in the manner employed by Korbin. It went beyond allowing the animals to thin out so the one doing the "cutting" could check on the brand each carried as they went by slowly. Delivered in such a blunt fashion, the implication was that the person to whom it had been made had deliberately allowed another's stock to become mingled with his own. In fact, bearing the suggestion of premeditated theft and there being nothing, except the purloining of a horse, regarded with such repugnance as a cow thief—the term "rustler" was not employed in the Lone Star State—it was seen as an insult by all Texans.

Although Stone and Waggles had no wish for hostilities to occur, they suspected something in that nature was being contemplated. Certainly the explanation given by Korbin could not be construed as a forthcoming demand for a "head-tax toll" before onward passage could be continued. There was, to the Texans' way of thinking, something of even more sinister import portended. Aware of how such a demand would be received, particularly when made to Texans—who had built up a reputation for resenting such a slur upon their integrity, even without as in this case the added inducement of the derogatory term "beefheads" and slighting references to "Johnny Rebs"—and willing to abide by the consequences, a rancher would be likely to take on hired guns rather than use his own cowhands to carry out his wishes.

Neither the trail boss nor his *segundo* would claim to be gunfighters, nor as well qualified in that respect as some of their friends, but each was aware that yielding mildly to the demand made by Korbin was not the solution to the situation. Either Wilson Eardle was ignorant of the way in which a request for the cutting of a herd would be received, or he was willing to provoke trouble by doing so. Whichever might be the case, the Texans knew yielding under what was clearly duress and permitting the inspection to be carried out would avail them nothing. Men like the Missourian in particular would see that as a sign of weakness and, even if they had been sent only to perform the task with no ulterior motive, that was almost sure to lead to further excesses.

The problem was that Stone and Waggles were badly outnumbered at the moment. The rest of the trail crew could reverse that aspect of the situation, but because none of them—with the possible exception of Silent Churchman, Peaceful Gunn, and Dude, all of whom were currently riding the drag—were any better qualified in matters *pistolero,* Stone had no desire to put them up against such opposition. What was more, despite the wagons having been halted and theirs being second in the line, his wife and Stephanie Willis were on hand, adding to his inclination to avoid trouble.

Not, the trail boss suspected, that he would be allowed to achieve this end. Every instinct possessed by Stone warned that the intention was to provoke hostilities—for some reason, other than a stronger-than-usual dislike of Johnny Rebs held by a die-hard Yankee, he could not understand.

With the declaration of intent so definitely made by

Korbin, the trail boss and his *segundo* knew that the matter was soon going to be pushed to a conclusion neither desired.

What happened next came as a complete surprise to everybody concerned.

"Seeing's how you don't cotton to Johnny Rebs," a voice that could belong only to a Texan and was menacing in its deep-throated timbre came from the concealment offered by the bushes, even closer than the spot where the bunch of hard cases had emerged, "Maybe you'd like to cut their throats while you're at it."

Although startled exclamations burst from the men confronting Stone and Waggles on hearing the words, none of them followed through on their intention of turning and dealing with the speaker. Before any of the actions could be completed, there was a very familiar-sounding mechanical double clicking that could be heard above the words. The distinctly menacing comments continued.

"This here's a Winchester Seventy-three I'm lining on you, *hombres.* She got seventeen flat-nosed bullets all ready to be turned loose fast and copious should they be needed. And they're going to be, if all them rifles aren't put back into their boots *muy pronto,* which means faster'n just lightning fast if you bunch of ignorant sons of bitches don't talk Mex. Should I need to start throwing said lead, *you'll* be the first to get it, tinhorn."

A low snarl of frustration left Korbin as he realized that the affair upon which he was engaged would no longer progress in the way he had envisaged to that point. The man by whom he was hired had stated that the idea was to provoke trouble for the Texans, and he had believed he was employing exactly the right means to bring this about. Nothing in the way the unsuspected interloper was speaking caused him to assume a bluff was being perpetrated—rather the opposite, in fact. There was a suggestion of Indian savagery under the drawled-out words that was chilling in its implications. No matter how he came to be in such an advantageous position, and Korbin had no idea by what means it had happened, that obvious son of the Lone Star State—albeit with the possibility of a mixture of racial blood involved—was clearly willing and able, as well as equipped, to exploit it to the full. The odds were still in their favor numerically, but that mattered little as long as he remained in his place of concealment and, as was most likely, he had a clear field of fire open to him.

From the speedy way in which the other men responded to the demand concerning their rifles—with one exception—Korbin concluded that they shared his opinion about the inadvisability of refusing to obey. He was not sorry to see that there was a general—but not complete—acquiescence and that the weapons were being slid back into the saddle boots from which they had been drawn back in the bushes. However, Robert "Skinny" McBride, who had injected the hurriedly revised comment about the feelings toward Johnny Rebs held by Wilson Eardle, did not comply.

"I don't have me a saddle boot!" the budding hard case asserted, confident the lie he was telling could not be detected from the unseen man's position.

"Then let that beat-up ole relic drop to the trail," commanded the hidden Texan. "Right *now,* or I'll fix it so you'll have to anyways. I wouldn't take kind' to thinking you'd been speaking an untruth about not having a boot, 'n' when I starts shooting, I won't be stopping until either I'm empty or none of you's left to need it."

"Do what he tells you and *fast,* damn you!" Korbin commanded savagely, having no doubt that the threat would be carried out and mindful that it had been said he would provide the first target. Then, as the Spencer rifle clattered to the ground, he tried to salvage something from what had become a most unsatisfactory situation. "Hey, trail boss, if there should be shooting, that herd of yours is going to stampede."

"You've got more to worry about from that than we do, seeing's how me and my *amigo* know what's coming should it start," Stone countered, knowing there was little chance of such a thing happening. The distance separating the cattle practically precluded a stampede, the weather had been mild for some time and nothing else had happened to disturb the even tenor of the march, and the cattle were not in the kind of nervous condition that was generally the cause of such a disaster. "You see, I've given my fellers orders that, should there be a stampede caused by something like this, they're to send it headed straight for whoever's causing the fuss."

"Which I'm for certain sure going to put at least some of you afoot afore them mean ole longhorns get here," warned the still-unrevealed speaker, having moved closer without being detected since his last comment. "Which *you're* going to be the first 'n' to go down, tinhorn. I can practical' guarantee that."

"And our boys're all ready 'n' waiting should they be needed to do as they was told," Waggles claimed, waving a negligent-seeming hand toward the herd. "Which is why-all the wagons've been stopped. We wouldn't want to chance nothing in any of them getting damaged in a rush, and anyways, our nighthawk's catching him some well-earned sleep in the bed wagon, so the boss's too kindhearted to want to have him disturbed."

Once again Korbin was faced with the unpalatable fact that his life would be the first endangered should a stampede start and be handled as the trail boss warned would happen. Concentrating on the two Texans who he had concluded were the leaders of the approaching herd, he had not noticed either the signal given by Waggles or the result it had produced. Now a quick glance informed him that he had been told the truth. There could be, he told himself, no other reason for the wagons being halted even though the cattle and *remuda* were being allowed to move onward.

No cowhand, preferring the less hard-worked life as a professional gambler to augment the earnings brought by hiring out his skill with a gun, Korbin had nevertheless heard enough about the dangers from a stampede to be aware of just how great a threat would be posed to those men left afoot by the unseen Texan. What was more, he did not doubt the warning that his would be the first horse shot. Faced with such a prospect and knowing his men were in no better position than himself to counter it, he accepted that there was only one thing left to do.

"All right," Korbin said with something closer to a snarl than a graceful acceptance of the inevitable. "You win, and even though Wilson Eardle's not going to forget what's happened when he hears, we'll be on our way."

6

IS THAT *YOUR* YOUNG 'N'?

"Hold hard there a minute, *Mr.* Korbin," Stone Hart said as the group of hard cases, the majority showing relief, started to turn away. "Seeing's how you've been sent to do a job, I reckon it's only right I should let you get it done."

"You mean you're going to let us cut your herd?" the gambler–cum–hired gun asked in tones of near-incredulity.

"The hell I am!" Stone replied in a most definite denial. Knowing he had established the point, he went on, "It's just that I was figuring on taking a trail count before we get to these bushes, and I don't mind you being alongside me so you can point out any of your boss's cattle, or from the other local spreads as they come through. You do that and I'll have any as comes fetched out so you can haul them back to the spread with you."

To anybody who knew the cattle business from a trail-driving point of view, there was a subtle distinction between allowing somebody to cut one's herd and permitting it to be scrutinized in a similar fashion under the pretense of carrying out a count of the herd as it went by. Jeremy Korbin was evidently aware of the difference and, although doing so would allow him to carry out his stated purpose, did not care for it. What was more, he felt sure that the offer had not been made out of fear of future reprisals. Rather, it was the means selected by the other for presenting him with a way to withdraw as if he had carried out the check by his own efforts. The gambler realized that to refuse might arouse unwanted suspicions on the part of the scar-faced Texan, who he concluded was a mighty smart man capable of drawing undesirable conclusions.

In one respect, the gambler had called the play correctly. The offer Stone made Korbin was in the interests of permitting him to save face.

It was possible, the trail boss had concluded, that Wilson Eardle was one of the increasing number of dudes who bought ranches west of the Mississippi River either as a sound financial investment or as a means of enjoying what they hoped would prove a more adventurous life than had been their lot back east. If such was the case, Eardle might not have realized that having a demand for a herd to be cut—especially in the way it was done by Korbin—was certain to be most forcibly rejected. Nor, wanting to earn fighting pay, would Korbin be likely to warn him of the danger.

Although the trail boss had tried along the way to learn more about the area in which he was to make his home, he had failed to increase his knowledge to any great extent. The route he had followed was selected to reduce contact with ranches from which stock might inadvertently become added to his herd, which also meant that it kept them away from any except the smallest villages. In those villages where he and his party had called, they had done so either to allow the men to relax for a while away from the cattle— which required so much of their time while on the move or bedded down at nightfall—or to pick up urgently needed supplies. Despite being pleased with the trade they brought in, the bartenders, storekeepers, and barbers with whom they had dealt disclaimed all except the most skimpy knowledge pertaining to the part of Arizona toward which the drive was headed. A couple of those questioned, being of Southron sympathies, had warned that the region was said to be a hotbed of Yankees unlikely to take kindly to Johnny Rebs intending to set up home nearby. In general, however, people appeared neither to know nor care about the subjects in which Stone was most interested.

Wanting to try to establish friendly relations with his neighbors, even though they could have served on the opposite side in the War Between the States and were perhaps disinclined to accept that it had ended several years back, Stone had concluded that the way he was acting would make a start in that direction. The last thing he wanted, especially since he had his and Rusty Willis's wives along, was to become embroiled in hostilities against the other ranchers in the vicinity. As he knew from all he had heard elsewhere, there was never a range war that did not leave both sides far worse off financially than when it started. Furthermore, with Arizona seeking advancement to statehood, becoming involved in one—even if it could be proved that the trouble was not of his doing or wanting—would do nothing to endear him to even the uninvolved population.

"Well," the trail boss said quietly after a few seconds had elapsed following his clearly unexpected explanation. "Do you want to play it *my* way?"

"Why not?" Korbin answered, conceding that nothing could be achieved at that moment toward accomplishing the assignment he had been given and hoping an opportunity would arise to do so while the counting of the cattle was taking place.

"Then let's get her done," the trail boss drawled.

"There's one thing, though," called the still-unseen

Texan from his place among the bushes. "Back home where I hail from in Texas, anybody as gets asked to do what you're doing is expected to show his good faith by standing on foot 'n' leaving his weapons on his saddle. My momma made me swear I'd allus see the same done, so I'll be obliged was you gents to do it."

"I would, was I you," Waggles Harrison declared, showing none of the amusement and delight he felt over the way in which the precaution was being demanded. "Ole Kiowa in there is mighty set in his ways and allus wants to do whatever his momma told him."

"Nobody's going to make me—!" Skinny McBride began, acting in the way that Korbin had expected would be the case sometime and offering the chance to provoke some trouble to serve their purpose.

"You wouldn't want to make a *liar* out of my momma, now would you, *hombre*?" challenged the mocking voice from the undergrowth. "'Cause a man could get hisself— and some of his *amigos,* or 'specially his boss—all bad hurt doing *that*."

"Play the way he says, damn you!" Korbin commanded, having decided that the time was not yet ripe for such behavior to prove advantageous and bearing in mind the warning he had received that he would be the first to suffer in the event hostilities of any kind broke out.

In addition to giving the order, the gambler set an example to the rest of his party by dismounting. After unbuckling his gunbelt, he hung it over the horn of the single-girthed Cheyenne roll saddle that identified him as one who had spent much time in the northern cattle-raising states east of the Rocky Mountains. Having done so, he glowered around to make sure that the rest followed his lead. Just as convinced that any attempt to refuse would be countered by painful and possibly lethal means, only one of the remaining hard cases did not comply exactly as was demanded.

"Hey, skinny-guts!" the concealed Texan called. "You must conclude your up again' another of your Missouri must-be-shown knobhead knobheads. When I said hang your weapons on your saddles, I meant all of 'em. Get that hawg-leg you've tucked under your vest all secret-like instead of leaving it safe holstered with its mate."

"Do it, damn you!" Korbin snarled, glaring to where McBride was registering consternation and alarm over his ploy's having been detected.

"Now, isn't that *nice,*" drawled the hidden Texan after his latest demand had met with compliance. "Does my li'l ole Texas heart good to meet up with such a real *obliging* feller."

With the disarming completed, the disgruntled hard cases left their horses hitched to branches of the bushes on the edge of the area in which they had found concealment. Then they were taken in the appropriate direction by Stone and Waggles. Looking behind as he was walking, Korbin failed to detect any trace of the man who had played a major part in the thwarting of his plans. Putting aside any thought of reprisals against the still-hidden Texan, he allowed himself to be led until he was standing with the other members of his party a short distance clear of the left side of the cattle. The position was selected as offering an opportunity for them to see the ownership brand every animal bore prominently on its near flank.

Before the first of the herd reached the standing men, the four wagons—which had been started in response to a signal to do so given by the *segundo*—began to pass. Except for Chow Willicka, who had a hefty and wicked-looking double-barreled eight-gauge shotgun resting across his knees, none of the wagons' occupants gave the standing men more than a casual glance. Sensing something of what had happened, the grizzled cook favored them with a scowl that somehow implied he wished for an excuse to cut loose with his weapon.

"Ama, Okie!" Stone called when he was sure his words could be heard and acted upon. "Make a trail count!"

Acknowledging the order with the traditional Cavalry—both Confederate and Union having used it during the War Between the States—response of "Yo!", neither of the men addressed gave the slightest indication of the surprise each felt over what they had been told to do. Instead, they immediately set off from where they were riding point on the massive and mossy-horned old *golondrino* that had served as lead steer on several drives. Advancing, they halted their horses a short distance apart in front of their boss, *segundo*, and the men on foot. With this done, allowing the open-ended reins to fall and dangle free, each removed a length of pigging thong from the pocket of his Levi's and hooked a foot up around the horn of his saddle to sit with an ease acquired from long familiarity with such a method.

Realizing what was intended, the next pair of riders passed the word back to the others spread along the flanks of the herd. Then, without any fuss or the need for further instructions, the experienced cowhands began to make it possible for the task at hand to be carried out. Until then, the cowhands had allowed the animals to amble along singly or in small numbers while remaining ready to counter any attempt by a group to break out in unison. Now they made sure that all were advancing in single file. Also drawing the correct conclusion on seeing what was happening, the wrangler slowed the pace of the *remuda* until the drag of the herd had gone by and followed in its wake instead of keeping parallel with the swing section to one side.

"One!" the two cowhands who answered to "Ama" and "Okie," respectively—the accepted abbreviations of the only names either ever gave, "Amarillo" and "Okla-

homa"—called simultaneously when "Ole Know-All," as
the lead steer was called, passed by.

Pure chance had found the two cowhands riding the
point that day, but Stone and Waggles could not have selected a better duo to perform the exacting task that lay
ahead. Each was older than the rest of the members of the
crew who handled the driving duties, and each had carried
out enough trail counts to be able to do so with considerable accuracy. Paying no attention to anything other than
the passing animals, they continued with their counting. As
every hundredth animal went by, each cowhand quickly
made a knot in his pigging thong to help with the final
reckoning. What was more, even though they had some
idea why the task was being performed, they instinctively
looked for any indications that a passing beast might be
sickening or had sustained an injury.

Also keeping watch for sick or injured animals, Waggles
did not forget the special reason the count was being made.
At his signal, two of the approaching hands drew rein and
received instructions for a special part they were to play.
Instead of continuing with their duties, they were to sit
their horses and prepare to extract any animal that did not
bear the brand of the Wedge. Waggles considered it a tribute to the efficient way the crew had performed their duties
that not more than half a dozen of the cattle in the first five
hundred to pass between the counters had to be cut out of
the line as the property of other ranchers.

On the other hand, the *segundo* was not oversurprised
when neither Korbin nor any of the other hard cases could
tell him more than the names of the men owning the other
spreads in Spanish Grant County. In fact, Waggles—and,
he suspected, his boss—would have been surprised if they
could have identified the initials AW inside a circle, the
logo by which Wilson Eardle for some reason established
ownership of his stock. However, the need for this did not

arise, since no animal so marked went by. The *segundo* guessed that there would not be any and that the demand to cut the herd for those that had entered either by accident or been put there deliberately had merely been a ploy to cause trouble for some reason.

Watching the number of cattle diminish as the counting continued, Korbin began to conclude that his chance of carrying out the task to which he had been assigned—and only he knew its real intention—was rapidly disappearing.

Then it seemed that the desired opportunity might be presented.

Looking around him instead of pretending to watch for Circle AW stock among the passing cattle, McBride, always a bully by nature but never of an observant disposition, saw something upon which he felt he could vent his anger over having failed to bring along the revolver he had concealed beneath his vest after obeying the order to leave his gunbelt behind. Approaching him was the short-of-stature cowhand, a calf being carried across his saddle.

Determined not to cause the slightest inconvenience to his charge, much to the unspoken amusement of Dude, Silent Churchman had ridden at a most cautious pace through the bushes in which they had had their dramatic meeting. Nor had he speeded up the gait of his kettle-bellied bay gelding more than enough to let him reach and pass along the flank of the herd in the direction of the blattin' cart when more open country was reached. He was further delayed when, despite being occupied in keeping the cattle in a line to permit the trail count to be carried out, the other members of the crew asked where he had acquired the calf.

After hearing the same story he was told twice—except that the supposed number of creatures that had threatened the deserted calf had increased—Dude had gone ahead to assist in the work being carried out. Making for the blattin' cart, the route Silent was of necessity taking caused him to come close to where the hard cases were standing. Instead of attempting to satisfy his curiosity, which was increased upon seeing that they were standing and had left their horses hitched some distance away, he made as if to go straight by.

"Hey, short-growed," McBride yelled loudly enough to draw every eye close by, except those of Ama—the nearer of the counters—in his direction. "Is that *your* young'n' you're toting? It sure looks *ugly* enough to be."

Which, as anybody who had made Silent's acquaintance for even a short time could have warned, was not the most prudent or safest way to address him.

Possessed of a quick rather than bad temper, the short Texan would not have permitted such a liberty to go unchallenged unless it was taken by a friend.

Belonging to a class of rangeland society for which Silent had no liking at the best of times, the lanky hard case most certainly did not fall into the category of friend.

"Your folks must've been *real* fond of children, or mighty short on having more worthwhile, to let you stay on with 'em," the stocky Texan replied, reining the bay to a halt. Running a gaze filled with disparagement over the hard case's scrawny frame, he continued, "Or did they keep the stork and send you back?"

"Why, you—!" McBride spat out as even some of his companions laughed at the spirited response. Following an instinctive reflex, he sent his right hand downward while going on, "I'll—!"

"You have to be wearing one to pull it," Silent pointed out as the hard case's fingers scrabbled at where the absent off-side Colt should have been. Then he gestured toward his holstered weapon without offering to touch its butt, and added, "Which same, I'm wearing mine."

"Call him off, Mr. Korbin," Waggles commanded as Mc-

Bride gave indications of launching a barehanded attack upon the Wedge hand. "Afore he gets chomped, whomped, 'n' stomped so fast he'll reckon the hawgs've jumped him. Which Silent's full capable of doing should he get pushed even a smidgen more."

"Stay put!" the gambler barked, and his moral ascendancy over the skinny hard case was such that his order was obeyed.

"Could be we'll meet sometime when I don't have nothing better to do, *hombre*," Silent drawled, starting the bay moving. "Should it happen, I'll be only too ready to go 'round the houses with you."

Although Korbin was carrying a Remington Double Derringer pistol in a concealed and readily accessible holster beneath his jacket, he did not know whether any of his men were armed in a similar fashion. Nor, since every Texan present and in the vicinity was openly packing iron, did he feel inclined to make an experiment to discover whether this was the case. Like every professional gambler he preferred to have the edge, and he was too uncertain of his position right then to take the chance.

A glance forward warned Korbin that the opportunity would not be granted in the near future. Standing by their horses, an Indian-dark and dangerous-looking man—obviously the one who had coppered their bets so effectively earlier—was engaged in unloading the weapons they had left behind and scattering the ammunition in the bushes with vigorous sweeps of his arm. Finding the means to reload the guns at that point would prove a most time-consuming affair, and to obtain a fresh supply from the nearest source would take even longer. Therefore, Korbin concluded that the only thing to do was forget his intentions and return for fresh instructions from the man who had hired him.

Ama and Okie concluded the trail count at the same

figure, and Stone insisted that Korbin sign—witnessed by two each of the Texans and hard cases—a document he had prepared. It stated that a check carried out in the gambler's presence had failed to produce any stock bearing the brand of the Circle AW ranch, and it was so worded that it would stand up if presented to either the local law-enforcement officers or the district court. With that precaution taken, Korbin and his men were allowed to go on their way.

7

MY DEAR HUSBAND
DISSUADED THEM

"What was all that business with the trail count about, honey?" Margaret Hart asked, having been informed by the driver supplied by freighter Cecil "Dobe" Killem to handle the wagon in which she and Stephanie Willis were riding that her husband was coming.[1] About the same age as Stone and five feet seven in height, although not classically beautiful, she made a comely sight. Clad in a gingham dress that was not sufficiently loose to hide the fact that she had a neatly rounded slender figure, with a plain white spoon bonnet covering tawny hair that she kept cut shorter than currently fashionable to facilitate keeping it tidy, she had features that the dark spectacles she wore to conceal her sightless eyes did not make any less attractive in their gentle lines. Mild though she looked, she possessed a strength of will and courage that had allowed her to come to terms with being blinded as a teenager and acquire skills making her far from helpless despite her condition. "Steffie says those bunch of hard cases you seemed to be doing it for didn't look any too pleased as they rode by."

"Could be they were disappointed we didn't have any of the Circle AW stock along," answered the boss of the Wedge crew and soon-to-be ranch in what he hoped would be taken for a nonchalant and uninterested tone.

Having dismissed Jeremy Korbin's party and seen them depart followed by Kiowa Cotton—who had, unbeknownst to them, done the same while they were approaching the herd and taking cover—Stone Hart had been satisfied that there was no way they could return without his being notified of their coming in time to make preparations to receive them. He had complete faith in the Indian-dark and dangerous-looking man General Ole Devil Hardin had sent unprompted to serve as scout for the drive in the absence of Johnny Raybold, who usually performed that function. He had met the replacement scout before on a couple of occasions, although they never worked together.

Satisfied that that aspect of the puzzling affair was in capable hands, Stone had gone with Waggles Harrison in the wake of the herd. However, knowing that his wife and her self-appointed maid-cum-housekeeper would be seething with impatience to discover what had caused the otherwise unnecessary work to be carried out, he had elected to ride ahead and settle their curiosity. Despite having attempted to relieve any anxiety they might be experiencing with the explanation, he began to form the opinion that it was not achieving the desired effect.

"Is that *all*?" Margaret asked, although the timbre in her Texas drawl made the three words sound more like a challenge.

"I've noticed that worthless man of mine gets all shifty, and butter wouldn't melt in my mouth when he thinks there's something I shouldn't know," Steffie remarked.

uneasy suspicion that it was not being received that way by either of the women. He had already come to know that his wife was a very discerning woman and well-versed in all aspects of life in cattle country, and he knew he was now receiving further confirmation of it. Since he still did not want to tell the truth for what he considered to be the best of motives, he concluded that there was only one honorable way of avoiding the issue for a Southron gentleman: make a passable excuse and get away *fast*. "Oh, blast it! I just realized I forgot to tell Waggles something, so I'd best go do it right now."

"Men!" Margaret snorted, but a smile played on her lips as she heard the sound of her husband riding away at a fair speed. "From what you told me, Steffie, that bunch wanted to cut the herd and my dear husband dissuaded them, probably with Kiowa's sneaky help, but he decided to make the trail count to let them save face and avoid trouble with their boss."

"I wish Rusty had that kind of tact," the ash-blonde stated, having no doubt she had heard the correct explanation.

"Don't worry," Margaret replied. "I'm sure *you* will soon have him that way."

* * *

"It's good of you to see me this late in the day, Counselor," Waggles Harrison asserted as the man he had come to visit in Child City, seat of Spanish Grant County, waved him and his equally travel-stained two companions into chairs on the other side of a large and tidy desk.

"That's all right, Mr. Harrison," Edward Sutherland replied, his Bostonian voice revealing just a trace of a Scottish burr. He was exuding the joviality that endeared him to most people who came in search of his legal services but had frequently caused his opponents in a court case to underestimate his ability until too late. Short and giving the impression of being chubby although his rotundity was produced by rubber-hard flesh, he had a sun-reddened face that seemed far more ingenuous than was the case. Waving a seemingly languid hand toward the door to his office, he went on, "I would have had to go in to the sitting room where my dear wife is holding a gathering of the good ladies in the Betterment of Child City League, and this gives me an excuse to put it off."

Despite the fact that Stone Hart had taken a hurried departure from the interrogation by his wife, the business he had gone to discuss with his *segundo* could not be carried out that day. Although it did not supply information about the location of the four ranches that had been formed when the property that gave the area its name was divided up following the death intestate of the original owner, the map they were using indicated that they were within the bounds of Spanish Grant County and that its seat was still too far away to be reached that afternoon. Therefore, it was not until the following morning that Waggles set off to have a meeting with the lawyer whose letter had informed Stone of his inheritance.

Bearing in mind the incident with the men claiming to be working for the AW ranch, and despite Kiowa Cotton's having returned toward sundown to say they showed no sign of returning to try to make further trouble, it had been decided that the *segundo* should not travel unaccompanied. He had selected Peaceful Gunn to be one of his companions, and with the agreement of the other regular members of the Wedge crew—one of whom would have been the other choice—decided to reward Thorny Bush's hard work and diligence throughout the journey by making him the other. Regardless of the paucity of other details given on the Army map of Arizona Territory by which Stone had guided them on the latter stages of the journey, they had had no difficulty finding the town, but the time was half past seven in the evening when they arrived at the office that was in the house owned by the lawyer.

"Well," Sutherland said, having examined the letter that Stone had given to Waggles. "In what way can I be of further service to Mr. Hart?"

"We'd like to know the setup in the county, among other things," the *segundo* replied, deciding that the jovial-looking—yet, he deduced, remarkably shrewd—lawyer could make a useful ally in the event of trouble forced upon the Wedge. "You see, the only map we've got is shy on just about everything 'cepting the shape of the old Spanish grant and how the town here's right smack in the middle of it."

"I can certainly help you there," Sutherland declared, and went to collect a rolled-up sheet of paper from an umbrella stand alongside a big filing cabinet. He unrolled it and held it flat by placing on it a couple of lumps of pyrite-streaked rock already on the desk. As he was doing so, he continued jovially, "I know they're only fool's gold, but I like to look at them and think what *might* have been when my wife bought them if they really had been genuine nuggets. Do any of you gentlemen have the pleasure of being married?"

"Not me," Waggles stated definitely, and medium-size, miserable-looking, heavily mustached Peaceful Gunn—who was armed with two Colt Civilian Model Peacemaker revolvers as well as a massive bowie knife, which he claimed were carried only to ensure that his pacific desires were respected—gave an equally vehement declaration of bachelorhood. "And Thorny here's a smidgen too young to make it."

"And aim to stay that way," Bush declared with considerable heat, despite being still somewhat overawed by the luxurious surroundings neither his home nor any other place he had been could equal.

"So did I, once," Sutherland said with a wry grin.

"Then why'd you get hitched—sir?" the youngster inquired before he could stop himself, adding the honorific in case he had caused offense.

"It seemed like a good idea at the time," the lawyer admitted with a grin. "And still does, except when the better half decides to have the Ladies Betterment of Child City League around. They talk worse than a bunch of senators and congressmen trying to think up more ways to get cash from their supporters."

"That's women for you," Thorny growled. "The way they talk—!"

"The way *you* talk, you'll be riding the blister end of a shovel when we get to the spread," the *segundo* warned, noticing that the lawyer appeared amused by the youngster's words. Then he looked at the map and found it to have more details than the one he had previously seen. "This is more like it."

"It was drawn up by a survey team of Army Engineers after the old don died intestate and nobody came forward to try to claim the grant," Sutherland replied. "The federal government had never been too happy about so much land in the U.S. of A. being owned by one man, a Mexican national at that. Only, it hadn't been considered good policy to chance riling the Mexican government by trying to dislodge him. And, with him dead and nobody else able to claim it, they decided they didn't want it all in a single person's hands again. So they took advantage of the geography allowing them to split it into four roughly equal-size parts with natural boundaries to delineate one from another. They were offered at public auction, and although I suspect it wasn't meant to happen, that was how Cornelius Maclaine got his part. Did you ever meet him?"

"Can't say as I ever had the *pleasure*," Waggles admitted,

remembering the less-than-flattering way in which the man they were discussing had been mentioned by his boss.

"You haven't missed anything," the lawyer asserted, drawing the correct conclusion from the emphasis given to the last word of the reply. "I trust your boss won't mind me saying that?"

"He said about the same thing," Waggles confessed without hesitation. "Fact being, he allowed he was tolerable surprised that he got left the spread."

"In my opinion, although I wouldn't care to be quoted verbatim or any other way on it," Sutherland intoned in his most impressively legalistic fashion despite there being a twinkle of amusement in his eyes, "the only reason Maclaine did so was that he couldn't take it with him or think of a way to stay on it. He neither said, nor did I feel it incumbent upon me to ask, why he left it to Mr. Hart. He certainly didn't give me the feeling he was doing it out of affection for a kinsman. His manner changed and his tone became more serious as he went on, "Now, how can I help you further?"

"Who runs the spreads?" Waggles asked, since the map did not give such information. Having noticed the frank way in which Maclaine had spoken, he had concluded that the question would not be regarded as out of order. "And, if you don't object, what kind of fellers are they?"

"Just so long as everybody knows what I say now will only be personal opinions," the lawyer said, but the *segundo* and older cowhand were aware that the warning was directed at their young companion, even if he did not. "Starting at the top and east, Patrick Hayes has the Arrow P. A New Englander, Massachusetts at a guess. He was one of the first to get his bid accepted and seems to know his business about running a ranch, although I don't know where he got his know-how. To the west is what its owner calls the Vertical Triple E on account of his name being

Egbert Eustace Eisteddfod, and he sounds like he originated in Illinois. Claims to be Welsh and talks it, but not on
Yum Kippur, I would say. In spite of his name I've never
seen him in church, and most Welsh folks I've known tend
to be religious. He was another of the first in. His friend
and his Cornelius Maclaine corraled the one below on the
west, using the C Over M as his brand. Feller called Loxley—sounded New York—!"

" 'Sounded'?" Waggles queried.

"He got the other at the same time," the lawyer elaborated. "But he died recently and it went to a cousin, Wilson
Eardle. I've heard that the aforesaid Mr. Eardle was a major with the New Jersey Dragoons in Arkansas and took
over the ranch a few weeks back. From what Shoey Dob-
son—he's town blacksmith and a damned good one—told
me while he was making the branding irons at his forge,
Mr. Eardle intends to swop the brand from the L Scissors
to the AW. I've not seen him so far."

"All those gents sound like they're Yankees," the
segundo drawled.

"They are, but so was Maclaine."

"The boss said so, allowed how Uncle Cornelius dis-
owned his momma 'cause she married a Johnny Reb and
raised her only son to be the same."

"The war's long over, Mr. Harrison."

"There's some—Gray 'n' Blue both, I'll admit—who
don't count it that way. How about around this way?"

"We don't have too many Southrons around the county,
but I've never heard of hostility with and from those who
are. Why did you ask?"

"Everybody who rides for the Wedge wore the Gray in
the War, or sides that way," Waggles answered. "Would
that be cause for making fuss with us 'cause we're settling
down here?"

"Not that I can visualize," Sutherland estimated with a

certainty that made the *segundo* assume he had already given the matter considerable thought. "And not from the townsfolk in particular. We all draw most of our living from the ranches, and your crew will be adding to it."

"How'll the other three ranchers feel, us moving in?"

"If they've any sense, they'll think you're an improvement on Maclaine. Anybody would be, comes to that."

"Was there any fuss between him and them?" Waggles asked.

"He didn't get along with *anybody,* but just out of his ordinary cross-grained nature," Sutherland answered. "But there was never any active hostility between any of them as far as I know, and a thing like that wouldn't have stayed a secret for long. Do you have any reason for asking?"

"Not 'specially," the *segundo* lied, but with the blandseeming veracity that made him such a capable poker player. "It's just we'd like to know the lay of the land, seeing's how we're moving in permanent 'stead of just coming to collect cattle to make a trail herd. Is there any trouble with cow thieves hereabouts?"

"None that I've heard of," the lawyer replied. "And I wouldn't say any of the ranchers would try it against the others. Going by what little I know on the subject, there's none of the brands which could be easily changed into any of the others."

"I'd say you know more than a little," the *segundo* praised, and he was genuine in it. Knowing the theft of cattle by one spread from others was frequently a bone of contention, he had been visualizing the way the local brands would appear and discounted the possibility on account of what he deduced.[2] "Anyways, as we'll be coming into town on paydays, how about the great seizer?"

"Amon Reeves is town marshal and sheriff combined, seeing as the county isn't rich enough to run to both. He wore the Blue, but you'll find he's a fair man and not like

Wyatt Earp and those other Kansas fighting pimps. You play square with him and hold the pay-night fun and games within reasonable bounds and he'll do right by you no matter which side you rode on during the war."

Considering what he had learned, Waggles remembered that the New Jersey Dragoons were one of the Yankee outfits against which the Texas Light Cavalry were in contention during the War Between the States. He wondered whether the newly arrived rancher might still harbor a bitter hatred against Southrons from something that happened in those days. That could account for why he sent men on a mission that he knew, or was told by Jeremy Korbin, could lead to gunplay and the scattering of a herd belonging to a Johnny Reb. However, sensing that Bush was getting restless and also not wanting to outstay his welcome with the lawyer, he decided against taking the matter up with the lawyer at that time.

"Well, I reckon we've taken up enough of your time," the *segundo* said. "I hope you don't mind me asking, but are you always so friendly with newcomers?"

"I am with *clients*," the lawyer claimed with a smile. "And don't get too grateful until after you've seen the account for this meeting I'll be sending to your boss. Do you know, the last time I sent one to E. E. Eisteddfod, he came asking why I'd billed him for two consultations. I replied, 'Have you forgotten you came back and asked if you'd left your pen behind?' "

"Am I right in reckoning Sutherland is a Scotch name?" Peaceful inquired dryly.

"It's *Scottish*," Sutherland corrected with a smile. "*Scotch* is a whisky."

"Which being, and the good ladies wouldn't object," the mournful-featured cowhand said, "as we've finished and all this chin-wagging's give' me a thirst, I don't suppose you'd care to show us someplace in town where we could have some of that same whisky to wet our throats? Just so we don't get billed for a consul—whatever you called it—for taking us to where it's at."

"Aye," the lawyer assented, sounding more Scottish than at any other time during the interview. "I think I can do that."

---

1. Cecil "Dobe" Killem makes a guest appearance in ARIZONA GUN LAW. More information about his career is given in the Calamity Jane series.
2. The brands of the ranches concerned are, respectively: Wedge, based on a splitting wedge; Arrow P; Vertical Triple E; C Over M, which Stone Hart had to replace with his own brand. Wilson Eardle's AW brand is self-explanatory.

8

WE HAVEN'T SETTLED THE RULES YET

"Hear me *good* and keep this in mind all the time we're in there, boy!" Waggles Harrison growled as Counselor Edward Sutherland was leading him and his two Wedge companions toward the front entrance of the Arizona State Saloon. "We all know as how Texas is the biggest and best damned place in the whole wide world and there're no cowhands anyplace as good as us Texans. Only, don't you go telling it when we get in there. We're just taking a couple of beers afore we start back for the herd and don't want to get into a fuss."

Reading the name of the establishment, the sign for which was lit by a couple of lanterns, the *segundo* of the Wedge had commented that the selection struck him as being a mite premature. Admitting that this was the case, the lawyer replied that the owner, Angus McTavish, was living up to the Scottish reputation for being "canny with the bawbees," since he knew the choice would not need alteration when that status within the Union was achieved.

While talking, having studied the number of cow ponies standing hip-shot and fastened to the hitching rail outside the building and its closed neighbors—their own had to be left across the street after being led from Sutherland's home, regardless of every cowhand's hatred for walking when it was possible to ride—Waggles had decided that the caution he had given was called for.

"I'll mind it *good*, Pappy," Thorny Bush promised.

"You'd *better*, boy," the mournful-featured older cowhand warned in a doleful tone of voice that seemed to quaver with anxiety. "'Cause I'm a man of peace and don't *never* take to having it spoiled by trouble 'n' fussing."

"My daddy allus told me you was just that, Peaceful," Bush claimed with a grin. He took no offense at either of his companions referring to him as "boy"; the way it was said implied they figured he'd right soon grow up and make a hand. "Fact being, he allows how you'd allus back off a good two inches from it if the river hadn't riz over the willows and there was no real easy crossing to hand."

Smiling at the reply from the youngster, which he concluded from studying and listening to the mournful-featured cowhand was a fair assessment, Sutherland allowed the trio to precede him into the spacious barroom. On entering and glancing around, he discovered that although none of the men he had hired to take care of what had been Cornelius Maclaine's property until the new owner arrived were present, there were representatives from the three other ranches that had been created out of the original Spanish grant. Apart from the absence of a contingent from the Corn spread, as it was known locally, the sight did not surprise him. It was payday and the various crews were in town to get rid of at least some of their hard-earned cash.

As Waggles entered and led his companions toward the bar, he too subjected the room to a careful yet unobtrusive scrutiny. He found what he saw far from disturbing. Apart from the possibility that the horses left before each of the three buildings belonged to different crews, it having been a matter of first come, first served when they arrived in town, there was no sign of segregation to the point where the different outfits formed their own groups. Rather, there appeared to be a general and amiable mingling that suggested no animosity existed between them. What was more, although he looked especially for them, none of the hard cases who had been prevented from cutting the Wedge herd were anywhere to be seen.

Before their party had reached the counter, the *segundo* concluded that the lawyer was a popular member of the community. While the three Texans were being subjected to a careful yet in no way openly hostile examination, cheery greetings were called to him from all sides. Further, space was made for Waggles to be able to make his order for them from one of the bartenders more quickly than he would have expected. As was required by range-country courtesy, they were allowed to sample their drinks before anybody showed more than a casual interest in them. Nor did any of the onlookers offer to make the first move in the matter of becoming acquainted. Not that there was need for this.

"Waggles," Sutherland boomed, using the *segundo*'s sobriquet instead of the formal "Mr. Harrison" for the first time. "I'd like you to meet with these good friends of mine. Steve Baird of the Vertical Triple E, Ed Leshin from the Arrow P, and Jimmy Conlin's the pride and joy of the AW, as it is now. Boys, get acquainted with your new neighbor, Waggles Harrison of the Wedge."

Even without the introductions, the *segundo* would have picked the men who moved forward as having the same status at their respective ranches. They wore the styles common in the northern cattle-raising states, with modifications to cope with the climatic conditions in Arizona. Their ages were around his own and, while of different heights and builds, each exuded the same kind of quiet and yet discernible authority. Competent and tough they all undoubtedly were, but there was no hint of the swaggering, gun-handy hard case about them.

"New neighbor, huh, Waggles?" Baird said in an accent that had its origins in Kentucky. "Would that be the C Over M?"

"Until we can vent 'em and give 'em our Wedge brand," the *segundo* replied, the question having been permissible under the code by which all of the group lived.

"I thought you Wedge boys only took herds on contract to Kansas," Leshin remarked. He sounded as if he hailed from Oregon.

"We've been a few other places," Waggles answered. "Fact being, we run one into Tombstone for the big Cochise County Fair."

"Now, wasn't *that* a whing-ding," Baird enthused, also exhibiting that he came from north of the Mason-Dixon line. "Even though he run some of us poor Northern boys ragged with his sneaky way of raiding in Arkansas, I forgave Dusty Fog for it when he took them fancy gold-mounted Colt Peacemakers Wyatt Earp was fixing to win."[1]

"Was I you, Mel," Conlin remarked in an amiable yet warning tone that had a timbre suggesting to Waggles he was more likely to have worn the Blue than the Gray if he had served during the War Between the States, "I wouldn't go talking too often about us poor Northern boys getting run ragged afore the new boss. He was there with the New Jersey Dragoons and is real proud of it."

"Cap'n Fog allus allows those Dragoons were the best he came up against all through the Arkansas campaign," Waggles remarked, taking notice that the foreman of the AW showed no sign of animosity toward him, or awareness that the plan to cause trouble for the Wedge had failed. Knowing nothing of the other's ability as a poker player, he could not decide whether the lack of reaction stemmed from an exceptional ability to conceal all emotion. "Fact being, he allows how one time a Yankee lieutenant he was escorting for a legal arranged trade for one of our'n escaped after giving his parole not to, and when a major in the Dragoons got told about it, he handed the cheating son of a bitch right back."[2]

There was more to the *segundo* speaking as he did than just a desire to prove he was on close enough terms to have heard at first hand of the incident from one of the South's top military raiders during the War Between the States and since had won acclaim as being an acknowledged master of the cowhand's trade. He wanted to get some idea of how his fellow foremen felt on the subject of the conflict. From what he estimated—and he had enough confidence in his expertise at poker to believe he could read at least some trace to supply a hint—none of them, not even Conlin, showed other than interest and perhaps approval for the behavior of the Dragoons' major in conforming to an accepted convention of war.

"The War's long over and best forgot, way I see it," Sutherland put in. "And talking about it's the thirstiest thing I know."

"I'll go along with you on that, Counselor," Conlin said with an air of tolerance that appeared to be genuine. "Likewise, I don't need the roof to drop in on me afore I can take a hint." Then he looked at the nearest bartender, a big and bulky man with a surly face who had contrived to do less work than the other two who were behind the counter, and called, "Hey, Mr. Medak, how's about setting up a round for us on me?"

* * *

"I tell you, boys," a young cowhand with a Kentucky accent announced to the other local cowhands gathered around, but with a pointed side glance at the two Texans. "It got so hot down here last *winter,* I sent a letter home to my folks in Knoxville and I was so dry I had to stick the stamp on with a pin."

"Do it get that warm back to Texas, friend?" an older man asked, in the fashion of one born and raised in Iowa, after the laughter in which the Wedge pair and everybody else in the vicinity had participated had died down.

"That's tolerable warm, I'll admit," Thorny Bush said, before Peaceful Gunn—to whom the question was directed—could speak. Wanting to meet what he knew to have been a challenge, Bush gestured with the half-empty schooner of beer purchased for him by his mournful-looking companion when they arrived, then went on, "But I bet you don't get the kind of *cold* we do back home to Texas comes late summer. Why, it gets so cold that you can't talk outside 'cause the words freeze solid as they're being spoke. The only way you can tell what's being said is to pick 'em up and go indoors to set 'em on the stove so's they can thaw out 'n' be heard."

Like Waggles Harrison, who was still engaged in conversation with the other foremen and Edward Sutherland, Peaceful was devoting his attention to studying the men around him. He had arrived at much the same conclusions as his *segundo* and could detect no suggestion of animosity toward himself and his young companion among the men from their level of cow-country society. In fact, it might have been a group gathered in any trail-end town saloon at the end of cattle drives. Wanting to learn more, he was not sorry that Bush had taken up what he, too, had realized was a challenge tossed their way. Going by the response to the story it was being well received, and he expected there would be attempts to top it. Nor was he kept waiting long for it to happen.

"You should go up 'round Flagstaff way for real cold," a third of the local cowhands suggested, he too sounding as if his sympathies would be those of a Yankee rather than a Johnny Reb. "We don't get any eggs for breakfast comes the middle of summer. The hens're so cold they try laying 'em standing up and they all get bust."

"That's surely cold," Peaceful conceded when Bush seemed at a loss for a way to produce a better story. "But I mind one time we was hunting up in the Texas Panhandle 'bout the start of the *one* day of summer we get there-abouts'd come. Found us a real ole grizzly b'ar a-hibernating—which is what real educated folk calls a-sleeping through the cold spell. Well, he woke up and would you believe he looks at us and says, 'Did they ever find out who chopped down Mrs. Martha Washington's cherry tree?'"

"There's one thing you can allus count on with beefheads and nothing else. They can come up with bigger lies than anybody else."

This came in what would almost certainly have been only a brief hiatus following the mirthful response to the latest piece of Texas wit, while the local audience were trying to come up with something to counter it; the words were spoken in a harsh and somewhat slurred voice having an obvious Northern intonation. They were delivered by a big and burly man with black hair longer than was considered acceptable by cowhands and framing a brutal, sneering face. He was clad in less-than-clean range attire, and the most noticeable thing about him under the circumstances was that he did not have a gun anywhere to be seen on his person. However, a knife larger than Peaceful's was sheathed on his waist belt. Teetering unsteadily, as if carrying more than a sensible quantity of bottled brave-maker, he gave the impression of having drunk not wisely but too well. For all of that, there were indications that he would be "dangerous when wet," as the saying went.

"Why, y—!" Bush began indignantly as silence began to descend over the barroom, starting to move forward with the intention of avenging the insult to his home state.

"Now, easy, boy!" Peaceful ordered, catching the youngster's right biceps in a grip like steel and bringing his movement to a halt. "You're too quick to temper. The gent's only exercising his rights under the Constitution of these here United States by saying what he did."

"Time was not long back you beefhead sons of bitches didn't give a shit for the Constitution, nor the *United* States," the burly man snarled, still swaying a little as he took a step closer to the mournful-looking Wedge hand.

"That was *way* back like you said, mister," Peaceful pointed out, giving the impression that he was close to being overawed by the other's menacing demeanor. "So there ain't no call to bring it up."

"Don't tell me what I can or can't bring up," the seemingly drunken man warned. "Even if you are toting two guns and I haven't but this here knife."

"Would it make any difference was I to take my guns off?" the Wedge cowhand inquired mildly. " 'Cause, 'cepting I'm a man of peace, I'd just natural' have to take you up on what you said about us Texans."

"Then shed 'em and pull out that big knife you're toting," the man suggested in a belligerent tone. " 'Cause it's been too long since I last killed me one of your goddamned yeller-bellied scum, and I'm fixing to change that right now again' you or that nose-wiping kid."

"You mean you want to *fight* me, with a *knife*?" Peaceful inquired, if such a term could be applied to the way his words sounded.

"That's just what I mean," the man confirmed.

"Then, much as I hate violence and such," Peaceful said, unbuckling his gunbelt and handing it to Bush, "I'm going to have to take you up on it."

"Who's that big jasper?" Waggles Harrison asked, watching what was happening, as was everybody else in the room.

"I've never seen him around town," Edward Sutherland stated, and the foremen of the local spreads murmured a similar lack of knowledge. Then, despite knowing that what he was going to say would be impossible under the code by which men like the leathery-faced Texan at his side lived, he went on, "Aren't you going to intervene?"

"Why should I?" the *segundo* inquired with no show of concern for the fate of his apparently very worried companion. "I've never seen that big son of a bitch afore, so why should I care what happens to him?"

"Hold hard, there!" Peaceful yelped in what appeared to be trepidation, as the burly man started to draw what proved to be a bowie knife with sawlike teeth in the back of its edge. "We haven't settled the rules yet."

Rules?" the man repeated. "You expect *rules* in a knife fight?"

"You mean there ain't any?" the Texan asked, looking more than a little perplexed and quite terrified.

"Of course there ain't!" the man confirmed, and glanced around to see what effect the conversation was having on the customers and saloon employees who were watching with rapt attention.

The action proved to be a bad mistake.

"Oh! Well, in that case—!"

Having gone no further in his comment, Peaceful changed from being apparently frightened and passive.

Instead of attempting to bring the bowie knife from its sheath on his belt, the Texan responded in a way that an expert at the French style of fist and foot fighting called *savate* would have considered masterly. Rising swiftly, the toe of his right boot passed between the man's obligingly—albeit inadvertently—parted thighs. Caught with considerable force on the most vulnerable portion of the masculine anatomy, the recipient of the attack gave proof of just how seriously he was affected. Agony distorted his already unprepossessing features and rendered them even less pleasant to see. Turning an ashen gray, eyes rolling back until only the whites showed, he collapsed to his knees.

However, the stricken man was not granted an opportunity to gain whatever relief might have accrued had he been allowed to move any further. For all that, he might have regarded the means by which he was prevented from doing so as something of a rescue from his immediate suffering. Pivoting rapidly and again with precision, his assailant sent another equally power-packed kick, only on this occasion the target was his chin. With his head snapping around under the impact, he was pitched onto his back, and as he descended the merciful blackness of an unconscious condition swirled in upon him.

"Well," Peaceful said, now speaking in an apologetic-seeming fashion as his would-be attacker quivered once, then went limp. "He did say there wasn't no rules."

"Give you one thing, *amigo*!" Bush enthused, returning the gunbelt to his companion without delay and showing a respect plain for all to see. "Pappy was wrong. You waited until you'd backed off a whole *two 'n' a half inches* hoping to stay out of trouble."

* * *

"Why did you let that long-haired bastard pull a stupid game like that?" demanded the shape that could only just be discerned as being masculine and whose voice, except that it had in all probability been east of the Mississippi River, was unidentifiable by accent yet held a timbre suggesting that it belonged to one long used to giving orders.

"His jaw's broken, from what I hear, so he won't be able to do what he's been brought and paid for to do."

"He come in the back way and said he wanted to take some liquor back with him," Peter Medak replied sullenly. The man he was addressing was speaking from the gloom of a dark alley, having attracted Medak's attention as the bartender was going to the accommodation he rented after the Arizona State Saloon had closed at the conclusion of a night's business, which—since he never cared to do any more work than was absolutely necessary—had been far too strenuous, to his way of thinking. "Didn't have no money. So, seeing as how the idea's to stir up trouble with the beefheads, I figured he might as well earn the price of his booze by doing something to help with it."

"You *thought*?" the shadowy figure snarled. "All your *thinking* achieved is that the beefheads still wound up leaving on good terms with the local cowhands, including the ones from my ranch, and Hayes won't be able to do what he was brought here to do for long enough that it will be of any use."

"You've said all along we should do something to cause trouble between 'em," the bartender repeated, unable to conceal the resentment he always felt when listening to the other, since he considered himself to be an equal partner in the enterprise upon which they were engaged, even though he had only recently arrived to participate. "Why didn't you send somebody to gun 'em down as they was headed back to their herd?"

"Who could I have sent, *you*?" the other man inquired savagely. "Korbin and his crowd are at my place and those six knobheads your bunch from back east sent weren't around the saloon, even if they'd have had the guts to take on something like that."

"I've been told to make use of them," Medak said in

tones implying a discounting of all responsibility for an error in judgment.

"Then you can put them to doing it starting tomorrow," the other man ordered. "Hart's going to need extra hands for the roundup he'll have to make if he's figuring to change brands on all of Maclaine's stock, which I'm sure is the case, as one of the men with Korbin who knows about such says his herd's all marked with his Wedge brand. Use them to see he doesn't get any, and make sure it's done the *right* way."

1. What happened at the Cochise County Fair is told in GUN WIZARD.
2. Told in Part Two, "A Convention of War," UNDER THE STARS AND BARS.

9

IT'S GONE'S FAR AS IT CAN WITHOUT KILLING

"I tell you, boss lady, boss," Waggles Harrison drawled at the conclusion of a brief description of the visit to Child City. "There wasn't a sign of any fuss going on between any of the crews, or not being taken with the notion of us Texans coming in to take over the C Over M. Nor of Jimmy Conlin, him being foreman of the AW, knowing what Korbin tried to pull on us comes to that."

In the cold gray light of dawn, the *segundo* was standing by the fire behind the wagon that carried the women and household items, cradling a large tin cup of coffee between his hands with a feeling of satisfaction over the warmth it gave to them. On the other side, a short distance away, Rosita and Miguel Vargas, the Mexican couple who ran the blattin' cart, and the cowhands who were not occupied elsewhere were gathered in a rowdy group around a larger blaze and eating the food that Chow Willicka served up in copious quantities. Ideas of class and racial distinctions did not cause the Harts to have their breakfast away from the trail-drive crew. Margaret had grown up around cowhands and had heard a variety of profanities inadvertently uttered by them in moments of stress.

Nevertheless, because of past experience, Margaret was aware that—contrary to growing tendency among middle class–middle management "liberals" to employ foul language in mixed company as an indication of a belief that doing so showed a willingness to descend to what they considered to be the usage of those less well educated than themselves in the hope of gaining a popularity that might produce the correct kind of voting in elections—the cowhands never deliberately offended, and invariably felt embarrassed over having inflicted such talk on the ears of a woman. They even attempted to avoid doing so with Rosita among them. Therefore, she, Steffie Willis, and the Mexican woman kept clear of their male companions at this always touchy time of the day.

On this occasion, aware that Waggles wanted to tell the Harts of what had happened in Child City the previous evening and that some of it might be of a confidential nature, the ash-blonde and her husband, who was always expected to join her unless he had not yet been relieved from his turn on the night herd, had gone with Rosita—to join the rest of the crew by the larger fire.

"How'd they take it after Peaceful had took up the toes of that jasper who picked on him?" Stone Hart asked, willing to accept the opinion of his range-wise *segundo* as being far more likely to prove correct than false.

"Made 'em even more friendly," Waggles replied. "Feller was a stranger to 'em on all accounts. Leastwise nobody up and said they knew him. Fact being, they reckoned ole Peaceful was right in forgetting his peaceable ways on account of how he got pushed into doing it. Why, they even forgive him for spinning that windy about the grizzly b'ar 'n' good ole Georgie Washington's maw, which takes some doing."

"Only if it's been heard as many times as we all have," Stone drawled with a grin. "Which, seeing as how this was your first time in Child City, they were fortunate not to have heard it even the once."

"I thought it was very funny," Margaret claimed. "The first hundred times I heard it, anyways. But, to get back to business, how did the marshal or whoever runs the law there feel about it?"

"Allowed Peaceful did what was best, him not being partial to having to move around jaspers who've been sli—!" Waggles commenced. "Anyways, the great seizer acts like he's a fair man and doesn't have no Kansas fighting-pimp way of thinking about us Texans. Which being, I'm going to tell the boys to keep that in mind and behave accordin' when we go into town after getting paid off for the drive. Which, I don't mind saying, I'm looking forward more'n a mite to. Everybody, 'cepting that poor jasper ole Peaceful abused so cruel, was so mighty friendly 'n' hospitable it surely was painful to have to light out as soon as we did."

"Sounds like you had a pretty enjoyable night of it," Stone remarked.

"I've had a whole heap worse," the *segundo* admitted. "And I tell you, boss, as well as being mighty helpful with what he told me, that Counselor Sutherland's as lively company as a man could ask for. Jimmy told me as how he whoops up a storm 'til the last dog's been hung 'n' it's pup's got shot on what he calls Burns's night."

"How did Thorny enjoy it?" Margaret asked. "I heard him going for breakfast, and he sounded a mite peaked."

"That's just tired, not 'cause he's got a liquor head," Waggles replied. "Give him his due, he stuck to beer and not so many of 'em was offered. Didn't rile nobody by saying no, neither. They all accepted as how we'd got a long ride back to the herd and it wouldn't be right 'n' fitting for the *segundo* not to be there to get the rest of the crew to working comes sunup. Anyways, he just come out with another of those jokes of his which is even *worse* than Peaceful's about the b'ar, and everybody allowed giving him more of it might make them even badder."

"Not that it's any of *my* business, before I get looks that say it," Margaret commented, eyeing Waggles in an apparently challenging fashion. "But I think he deserves something *nice* for doing it."

"And something *nice* is what he's going to get," the *segundo* promised, showing no offense over the interference with his duties, not that any had been expected.

"And just what might *that* be?" Margaret inquired suspiciously, her knowledge of the speaker's sense of humor causing her to draw a conclusion from the way in which the declaration was made.

"Figured I'd send him off with Silent to see if they can pick up any C Over M stock and fetch it with us to be rebranded," Waggles explained.

"I'll bet Rosita's pleased that Silent's not going to be around for a spell," Margaret remarked. "She says he keeps hanging around that Hereford calf he claims he saved from five grizzlies, three cougars, twelve of the biggest black bears he'd ever seen, and a jaguar like he was its pappy."

"Seems to me that li'l calf needed saving from more of 'em every time I hear 'bout it," Waggles drawled. "Which, if there's nothing more you want to know, boss, I'll go 'n' 'tend to it right now. Blast it, the day's more'n half gone and nothing 'cept feeding their faces like they're scared eating's going out of fashion, has been done yet."

Nodding his head at Margaret, who guessed this would be done and responded with a quick curtsy, the *segundo* strolled toward the main fire. As he came up, he discovered

that either Peaceful Gunn or Thorny Bush had been re-
counting the events of the previous evening to the others
assembled at it. From what was being said by one of the
cowhands, there had just been some reference to the owners of the neighboring ranches.

"Eisteddfod, is that what you're trying to say?" queried
David Montgomery. His Texas drawl had a somewhat lilting
timbre indicative of the Welsh origins in which he took
great pride.

"Why, sure," Peaceful confirmed. "That's how Counselor Sutherland said it."

"Then the man isn't Welsh, look you," Montgomery asserted. "The Eisteddfod is our most sacred occasion, not a
family name."

"Said Counselor did hint such could be," the mournful-
featured cowhand admitted, then turned his gaze to the
segundo. "Morning, Waggles, it's sure nice to see you about
so good 'n' early."

"This isn't what I call early," the *segundo* growled with
mock ferocity. "It's near to noon, and I thought as how
Chow'd started serving a fancy dude lunch."

"You mean as how you reckon we should be doing *something*?" Peaceful asked in what appeared to be a solicitous
fashion, glancing around to where—like himself—everybody else was close to finishing their breakfasts.

"You just *had* to ask," Silent Churchman growled at the
doleful one after Waggles had given instructions for the
work to be performed. "I thought we'd be allowed to stand
about whittle-whanging for at least another hour."

* * *

Seeing and recognizing the man who had appeared as he
topped the latest ridge he was traversing, Silent Churchman was not sorry he had drawn his Spencer carbine from
its saddle boot on coming across the tracks of what he

concluded from the size and other indications were recently made by a good-size deer or even an elk.

The task to which Silent and Thorny Bush had been assigned by Waggles Harrison had proved moderately productive. Only an hour had elapsed and they had gathered almost enough cattle bearing the C Over M brand to make a return to the herd advisable. Moreover, they had found enough evidence to suggest that the range Stone Hart was going to call his own was well-stocked. With that possibility in mind, the stocky cowhand had decided to leave his young companion to hold the gather while he made a quick scout of the immediate area to see if more definite proof would be presented. He had also hoped there might be an opportunity to collect some game meat to make a change from the beef that had been the main item on the menu since the last time hunting had been successfully carried out. The tradition that whoever fetched in a dead animal received first choice of its meat when cooked was a prime inducement.

The last thing Silent would have expected to come across was a member of the bunch of hard cases who had tried to cut the Wedge herd in the vicinity. Having continued to keep a careful watch, Kiowa Cotton had not mentioned finding anything to indicate that they were still around. Not only did the chance meeting fill the stocky cowhand with a sense of grim foreboding, but he was able to identify the man as the one with whom he had exchanged a few unpleasant words as he was passing with the calf headed for the blattin' wagon.

Going by the response that was given in acknowledgment of his own presence, Silent assumed the recognition was mutual.

Ever since his companions had seen him compelled to "back water" from the smaller Texan while the trail count was forced upon them, Skinny McBride had been the subject of much derision from them. It had rankled to such an extent that he had stated his determination to go back and finish what was intended. His hope of having some of the others accompany him had come to nothing. Even Jeremy Korbin had refrained from making the offer, not that McBride would have wanted him along, since Korbin was sure to claim any credit that might accrue from a successful completion of the scheme.

Belatedly remembering the efficient way in which the Indian-dark and dangerous-looking Texan had prevented them from carrying out their intentions, the scrawny hard case had been aware of the risks he was running. Therefore, he had selected a route by which he hoped to evade the other's scrutiny and bring him up to the herd from the rear, as it was possible that no danger would be anticipated from that direction. Without realizing that the sensation was mutual, he had been surprised to find himself face-to-face—albeit still at a distance—with the cause of his humiliation. However, he saw a way by which he could produce a result without incurring the added risk of going to the herd to bring it about.

"Hey, you short-growed Wedge son of a bitch!" McBride bellowed, too eager to put his idea into effect to study the stocky Texan carefully. Shifting the Spencer rifle into a better position of readiness across his knees and drawing the hammer back to fully cocked, confident he was too far away for the clicking to be heard by his intended victim, he continued, "What're you doing out this ways, looking to wide-loop some more of our AW cattle?"

"The boss's real choosy about what kind of beef he lets come into our herd," Silent shouted back. "Which being, he wouldn't give any stock the likes of you've had a hand in raising within a good country mile of our'n."

"You beefheads'd steal anything that wasn't roped down

good and tight!" the scrawny hard case asserted, and began to lift the Spencer rifle toward his shoulder.

Just an instant too late, McBride realized that his intended victim was armed in a similar fashion.

Alert for trouble, and having noticed the hard case's rifle in a position of readiness, Silent had made preparations for applying defensive measures while the conversation was taking place. Because he had anticipated having to make a speedy shot at whatever animal had made the tracks, both deer and elk being noted for possessing wary natures and a strong disinclination to having human beings anyplace around them, he had coiled the open-ended reins around his saddle horn to allow his hands to wield the carbine. Although he was not riding the kettle-bellied bay that was his favorite, he was confident the spot-rumped Appaloosa gelding selected that morning from his mount was just as steady and suitable for his present needs. He was aware of how much time was needed to bring the Spencer carbine to an operative state, so he was carrying it with its action fully cocked.

At the first indication that the other was planning to commence hostilities, Silent retaliated with the speed of long practice. However, his bullet passed harmlessly over McBride's head. An instant later, the delay resulting from the weapon's greater length in spite of the move having been started a fraction before that made by his intended victim, lead from the hard case's weapon—which he identified as being one of the rifle version of the same make as his own—stirred the right sleeve of his shirt as it winged by.

Each starting the task of reloading his weapon, the two men instinctively nudged their horses into motion so as to reduce the distance at which they would fire their second shots. Although the rifle being handled by the scrawny hard case had the greater potential for accuracy, the carbine held by Silent was less cumbersome; he was also the better-mounted man.

Unused to having firearms discharged so close above its head, the animal ridden by McBride began to fiddle-foot nervously at the worst possible moment. In such circumstances seconds were of vital importance, and as it was often said, there was no second-place winner awarded in a gunfight. Before he could regain full control of himself or his horse, he saw with a sickening sense of alarm, the carbine being lined with disconcerting—even frightening—steadiness toward him. However, when it went off, he might have counted himself fortunate. Showing its resentment, the animal tossed its head just as the weapon cracked for the second time. Struck there by the heavy-caliber bullet, it was killed instantly and crumpled down as if it had been suddenly boned to roll onto its side. After kicking spasmodically a couple of times, it went still.

Impelled by the speed of desperation, retaining his grasp on the rifle more by luck than deliberate intent despite the recoil kick, the hard case contrived to throw himself clear just in time to avoid having a leg trapped beneath the collapsing animal. Still being driven by a close-to-overwhelming fear of the consequences to move faster than would have been the case in less dangerous circumstances, he wriggled until he was able to crouch behind the carcass and began to recharge his weapon.

Also replenishing the chamber of his carbine, Silent surveyed the situation and decided he did not care for the way it had developed. Not only had he killed the horse without injuring its rider in any way, but the latter was now in a most adequate position to cope with any further measures Silent cared to take. In going down, by pure chance the animal had descended into a shallow coulee, an additional shelter to that provided by the horse's body. All of which meant, the stocky cowhand conjectured with some bitterness, that the man was in a position from which he could shoot without needing to show much of his body. Furthermore, as Silent had noticed with annoyance, he still held his rifle, which had the advantage in range over the shorter and more compact carbine.

As if reading Silent's thoughts, McBride began to raise himself cautiously into the lowest possible position from which he could take aim and limit the target he was presenting. Seeing this, never being so foolhardy as to expose himself to the weapon of a desperate man—especially one he suspected hated him—when it possessed a potential greater than his own, the stocky cowhand decided that discretion was the better part of valor. Releasing the carbine with his left hand, he made a derisive gesture and swung the Appaloosa to send it loping off in the direction from which he had come. He never discovered that he had a piece of luck.

Snarling profanities as he watched his intended victim turn and ride away, McBride aligned the rifle with all the skill he could muster.

When satisfied that its sights were aimed at the Texan's back where it would deliver a fatal wound rather than kill instantaneously, the hard case squeezed the trigger.

Nothing happened!

In his eagerness to take revenge upon the Texan who had added injury to insult by killing his horse, McBride had forgotten that the rifle had been fired before he went down and had failed to reload it.

By the time the hard case had corrected the mistake, the other man would be beyond any range at which he might hope to make a hit.

There was something even more alarming for McBride to consider. Even as he was about to lower himself to complete shelter behind the horse, he saw a younger Texan riding over the rim ahead of the first. With a sickening

sensation in his stomach, he realized that his erstwhile se-
cure position had suddenly become exactly the opposite.
Until the newcomer appeared, he had comforted himself
with the thought that the worst the stocky cowhand could
do was ride around in an attempt to take him from a position where he would not be hidden by the dead horse.
Before this could be accomplished, he would have been
able to slip across the carcass and adopt a similar position
of safety on the other side. But keeping at a distance beyond the range of his rifle, the pair of them could time their
tactics in such a way that one could move in close enough
for his shorter-range weapon to make a hit upon him while
the other held his attention in another direction.

"What's doing, Silent?" Thorny Bush demanded, reining
his latest paint to a halt. "Why all the shooting?"

"It's one of Korbin's bunch," the stocky Texan replied. "I
had some fuss with him while the trail count was going on,
but it didn't come to nothing more'n him spitting out words
to see if he could make 'em splutter."

"So he's come looking for evens?" the youngster suggested.

"Could be," Silent admitted. "But he allowed he figured
I was out looking to wide-loop some of the AW's cattle."

"Are any of his bunkies 'round?" Bush asked, bristling
with belligerence.

"Wouldn't say so, what I've seen of him. He'd never have
made his play lonesome had there been more of 'em
around."

"What say we start figuring some way to hand him his
needings?"

"Nope."

"NOPE?" the youngster almost howled.

"Nope!" Silent confirmed emphatically. "There's no
harm done to me and it's gone as far as it can without
killing, and the boss don't want none of that."

"Have it your way," Bush said with a sigh. "You most times do."

"My way's allus the best," the stocky cowhand claimed with what sounded almost like modesty. "If there's more of 'em around, they ain't real close or Kiowa'd've found 'em afore now. Which being that skinny son of a bitch has got him a fair way ahead of him to join 'em, and he'll have to do it *afoot*."

"There's that," Bush conceded. "Only, I hadn't aimed to mention it, but I don't reckon there was more'n a round dozen grizzly b'ars and wasn't no jaguar to hand when that li'l ole calf rescued you. Come on, let's get back to that gather I've made afore they scatter all over the range again."

10

I KNOW IT, YOU KNOW IT,
BUT DOES MR. EARDLE?

"So that scrawny *hombre* reckoned you were trying to wide-loop AW beef, did he?" Stone Hart inquired.

"That's what he reckoned," Silent Churchman agreed, having reported what had taken place during the lastest run-in with Skinny McBride after rejoining the herd with the C Over M cattle he and Thorny Bush had gathered. "Could be it was more 'cause he was riled up over what came off when we was like' to lock horns on the trail count, and was hunting for evens."

"'Cepting he wouldn't've figured on finding you where you was," Waggles Harrison pointed out. He had received a signal to leave the point of the herd and join his boss to hear what the stocky cowhand had to say. "Not unless he'd been scouting the herd and seen you light out with Thorny. Which being, he'd have to've been smarter'n he struck me as being to have done the scouting. I'd say even Johnny'd've been real lucky to pull off a scout and Kiowa not find him. Fact being, I only know one feller who could, and I wouldn't say that skinny *hombre*'s another Ysabel Kid."

"There's them's've said just *one* of the Kid's *four* at least too many," Silent drawled, unable to stop the kind of comment by which a cowhand indicated he had the greatest admiration for the man about whom he was speaking. "And, at the risk of being thought an apple polisher, which everybody knows I *am,* I go along with you about that knobhead not being one of 'em."

"Seeing as how he almost certainly wasn't hunting you special for evens," Stone remarked, "why'd he reckon you was after wide-looping AW cattle?"

"Could reckon everybody's mean, dishonest, 'n' sneaky, as he knows he is," Silent offered. "And, which I wouldn't put past him no more'n I would hearing he votes Republican, being the sort he is, he's likely done a fair amount of wide-looping 'n' concludes everybody else's the same."

"Except, unless that map Counselor Sutherland sent along is wrong," Stone countered, "we're just about off AW range, and that puts us on our own. Sure, I know them goddamned cows you hate so much don't have a lick of enough good sense to know where they should be. Only, I wouldn't've thought a yahoo like him would be so all-fired keen to earn his pay that he'd be riding on speculation looking for some of us fixing to wide-loop some of his boss's beef."

"Could've been told to go out 'n' do it," Silent suggested, and closed both eyes before continuing. "Present company not counted as such, way I see it, there's *some segundos*'re real mean like that."

"Why'n't you go look in on that little ole calf who saved you from all them fine critters?" Waggles growled. Then he went on in a less annoyed-sounding manner, "Like I said this morning, boss, nothing I saw of Jimmy Conlin makes me think he'd pull a game like sending somebody to make fuss with us. Or, if he did, after what happened when they made their try, he's smart enough to've picked somebody a heap better than that scrawny *hombre*. There's another thing: none of the crew he had with him came close to being from the same litter as Korbin 'n' his bunch. They was all cowhands no better nor worse than any others I've come across saving these yahoos I've got saddled with. *Anybody'd* have to be better than *them*."

"He means *us*, your loyal, faithful, 'n' hardworking crew, boss," Silent informed his longtime employer as if wishing to let him in on a carefully kept secret.

"And I'm inclined to reckon he's more right than wrong on it," Stone declared, then became serious. "Anyways, *amigo*, I'm right pleased you didn't kill him."

"Got to thinking as we was headed back as how we should maybe've brought him in so's he could do some talking," the stocky cowhand admitted. "They do say ole Kiowa runs the Kid close second on persuading fellers to speak up all free 'n' helpful. Which some of us aren't exactly slouches at it, neither. Only, he'd got him a Spencer *rifle* again' me 'n' Thorny toting carbines, so doing it wouldn't've been easy."

"And as much shooting as it'd've likely took," Waggles drawled, knowing Silent would not have been deterred by the possible danger—other than on Bush's account—if he had thought the attempt would prove productive. "Any of his bunch who might've been around'd've come a-running even if they didn't like him, and nobody could blame 'em should that be the case. Then you'd have had you a shooting war on your hands, boss, which none of *us* wants."

"I know it, you know it, but does Mr. Eardle?" Stone said soberly. "Because, way everything's starting to look, it seems like he's hunting fuss regardless of what you reckon about his foreman and crew you met in town."

*   *   *

"Do you reckon you'll like it here, honey?" the boss of the Wedge asked in the kind of worried tone a husband always adopts when his wife is about to make the first acquaintance with what is to be her new home.

"I'm sure I will," Margaret Hart replied, only just refraining from adding, "because we'll be there together." Instead, having no desire to appear as romantic as a young bride after having been married for—well, too long for such to be considered fitting, she went on, "Steffie's described it for me, and it sounds just like I've always dreamed of living in."

Glancing at the tawny-haired woman by her side, Steffie Willis was hard put to hold down a smile. She would not, she told herself, ever have let it be known how she harbored a similar affection for her husband of a slightly shorter period.

Because Kiowa Cotton and the rest of the crew had maintained an even closer watch after the incident between Silent Churchman and Skinny McBride—perhaps even because of it—the last remaining miles of the trail drive had passed uneventfully.

On coming into sight of the property that was to be the permanent home for the Wedge, Stone Hart had left dealing with the herd to Waggles Harrison and ridden to where the line of wagons was approaching. Calling a mock-derisive warning to the big Chesapeake Bay retriever loping alongside his wife's vehicle that its days of loafing around hunting rabbits were over and it would be back to serious work again, he received a wag from its tail. Then, anticipating Steffie would have supplied the necessary information about the ranch's buildings, he had addressed the question to Margaret. In fact, as he rarely gave a thought to Margaret's being blind—so competently did she comport herself in everyday life—he had only just prevented himself from phrasing the question as if she could have made the examination herself.

Paying more attention to what lay ahead than he had so far due to his being absorbed in the preparations for the disposal of the herd, Stone studied the buildings and their surroundings. He decided he liked what he saw and felt sure the ash-blonde had described them accurately for his wife. As he felt sure would be the case with every ranch in Arizona Territory, the threat of Apache raiding never entirely dying away regardless of whether there were any in the vicinity or not, the buildings were laid out in a position that allowed each to offer mutual defense with the others. Most headquarters for spreads in the Lone Star State were erected in a similar fashion for the same reason, although Comanches, Caddoes, and Kiowas were the primary cause after the threat from *Comancheros* had been brought to an end by a most effective punitive action, carried out primarily by the Texas Rangers.

Set as the central point of the layout, the ranch house could not come anywhere close to matching the size and elegance conveyed by General Ole Devil Hardin's enormous OD Connected spread in Rio Hondo County. Stone had visited it for social reasons on several occasions—it being large enough and sufficiently prosperous to send its own trail herds to the shipping points in Kansas—and he had received the kind of hospitality for which it was justly famous throughout Texas. In fact, he felt it could be a touch too small for what Margaret and he had in mind as being part of their not-too-distant future. Shortly after their wedding, they had been assured by a young doctor freshly arrived from the East and well-versed in all the latest medical techniques and discoveries that her blindness was unlikely to be passed on to her offspring. Therefore, they had decided they would make a start at raising a family once the Wedge had come to its permanent home.

From the study he had made while coming to joining Margaret, Stone concluded that it was not only the size of the house that would need to be enlarged. Whereas the barn and small blacksmith's forge would be sufficient for their needs, the two corrals could do with being made larger. On the other hand, because he would only be retaining the permanent members of the Wedge crew for the everyday handling of chores and taking on such additional help as was required for such things as a major roundup on a temporary basis, the bunkhouse—which he guessed had a kitchen for Chow Willicka to lord over attached—would be adequate, although he had no intention of restricting the standard of their accommodation to what it was claimed was once offered by the so-called Cattle King, John Chisum.[1] He was also pleased to notice that there were two smaller buildings, apparently equally sturdily constructed, which would serve as living quarters for Steffie and Rusty Willis and the Mexican couple, who would also be staying on. To further make the property attractive from his point of view, the grazing around it was good and what he guessed from some trees and bushes growing along the banks would be a permanent stream flowing in a curve around the buildings and which had been dammed to form a good-size pool that would be ideal for watering stock.

All in all, the boss of the Wedge considered himself fortunate in his inheritance.

However, Stone still felt puzzled over why Cornelius Maclaine—with whom his mother had always said they had never been on friendly terms—had elected to leave him such an obviously valuable property.

"What's going to happen next, now we've got to our new home, honey?" Margaret inquired, cutting in on her husband's reverie.

"We'll leave the herd to graze 'n' rest up 'round here and get ourselves all fancied up—!" Stone began.

"Oh, that's just for you *men*," Margaret stated, contriving to sound as if the disposal of the animals upon which to a large extent the future of the ranch depended were a matter of minor importance. "I mean in the *house*."

"Well, now," Stone answered with a grin he knew his wife would sense even though she could not see it. "I'd say as how, being right uppity for a new' wed, and be a real respectful wife is a chore for you, Steffie and Rosita and such being so's makes it none of my never mind."

"I do so wish that fool Rusty of mine was as smart and knowing as your catch, Margaret," the ash-blonde declared. "At least he knows what's what."

"It took me a long time to train him that way," the tawny-haired woman asserted. "And Mr. Stone Hart, I'm not all that new' wed. Anyways, what's coming next?"

"I'm going to pay off the crew 'n' let them go into town for a whing-ding like has always been done at the end of a drive," the boss of the Wedge replied.

"Will the herd be all right when you've gone?" Steffie inquired. "And, afore *I* get told, that's no never mind for us womenfolk."

"You're right, likely for the first in your life 'cepting when you let Rusty do you the honor of being his wife," Stone answered. "But they've been traveling a good spell without more resting than was got overnight. So, being the grazing 'n' water's good right here, they won't figure on doing much moving around." He paused and waved a hand toward where an elderly-looking woman and four men of around the same age were coming from the front door of the ranch house. "Here come the folks Counselor Sutherland took on to watch over the property until we got here. Likely those gents can do all the 'tending all the herd'll need 'til the boys come back."

"Don't you mean 'the boys and I get back,' dear?" Margaret asked. "I've heard you always go with them on the first whoop-up at the end of a drive."

"Sure I used to," Stone admitted, as his wife had spoken the truth about his invariable habit when reaching the destination after a trail drive. "But—!"

"There isn't any 'but' about it," Margaret declared in a firm tone. "I know you're going to be a regular henpecked husband, but I don't want you to find it out just yet. So you're going and Steffie and I have a few things we want to get from the general store, so we'll come along. There's sure to be a hotel or somewhere else we can stay until you menfolk get through drinking and carousing."

"Have it *your* way, honey," Stone drawled, guessing that his wife and the ash-blonde were not averse to the chance of getting away from the cattle for a while.

"I *always* intend to," Margaret threatened.

"The great seizer's headed in, boss," Waggles Harrison reported, riding up before any more could be said. "I wonder what's bringing him here?"

"Not to throw all you worthless bunch in jail before you can lead that sweet innocent husband of mine astray, I don't suppose," Steffie remarked. "I just couldn't be that *lucky*."

"Now me, I thought you married *Rusty*," the *segundo* countered. "Anyways, boss, he's likely only drifting over to let us know when the next lot of taxes on the spread'll be coming due."

Studying Amon Reeves as he rode closer accompanied by an Indian-dark and slightly surly-seeming young man wearing the badge of a deputy sheriff, Stone concluded that he was the kind of peace officer Waggles had claimed. Tall, well if not bulkily built, there was nothing of the swaggering bully the Earps and others of their kind displayed. Furthermore, his clean range-country clothing was of a sufficiently moderately priced kind to imply that he was honest enough to live on just his salary as sheriff. While there was strength in his not-unpleasant tanned features, there was also a suggestion of the saving grace of humor. Such a man, the boss of the Wedge knew, would handle his duties fairly and well. The walnut-handled Colt Peacemaker revolver on his right side hung ready for rapid use, and he gave the impression of being capable of making the best of this advantage.

"Howdy, Cap'n Hart, ladies," the sheriff greeted as he and his companion drew their horses to a halt a short distance from the wagon. His accent was that of a New Englander in spite of his appearing completely at home in his Western clothing. "Mind if me 'n' Deputy Alvord light and talk a spell?"

"Be right gratified if you would," Stone authorized, pleased by the display of correct range-country etiquette, which some peace officers would have ignored.

"I'm afraid we don't have any coffee or food to offer you, gentlemen," Margaret apologized in her capacity of the woman of the house, even though she had not yet been inside it. "But if you can wait a little while, I'm sure some can be fixed."

"My thanks, ma'am," Reeves replied, doffing his hat before dismounting. "I'm right sorry, but I've a mite of business to do afore I do any sociabilizing."

"Which means you don't want any nosy womenfolk around," Margaret said with a smile. "So we'll go and see if we can scare up the coffee and a mite to eat."

"Well, I'll be switched!" the sheriff exclaimed, as the wagon started moving and, having been standing in a clearly protective posture below its mistress, the big dog went along with it. "I haven't seen a Chessy in more years than I want to think on. How is he on fetching back ducks?"

"He's never been tried, but he's slicker than a chicken hawk with four feet on rabbits," Stone replied, and seeing a brief expression that passed over Reeves's face, continued in a tone redolent of apology, "If that doesn't make a duck-hunting man like I figure you to be feel like throwing up. Now what can I do for you, Sheriff?"

"It close to does," Reeves claimed with a grin, then became serious. "Anyways, I had a feller with a complaint come into the office soon as I opened her this morning. He allows that he was riding along peaceable and minding his own business when he come across two of your hands with a herd of cattle. Was figuring to go on by when damned if one of 'em didn't up 'n' throwed down with a rifle and shot his hoss from under him. Did it happen that way?"

"Not as I was told by the hand, who I'll come out straight and admit did shoot his hoss from under him," Stone answered, drawing a conclusion he regarded with offering to lead to satisfactory relationship with the sheriff, going by the way in which the question was posed after the brief digression concerning the Chesapeake Bay retriever. "Way Silent tells it, he was hunting for some more C Over M cattle to add on to the gather him and another of the crew made so's we could vent and rebrand them with the Wedge when he come on that scrawny *hombre*. They'd had less'n friendly words last time they met and the jasper took to talking mean, then cut loose with a rifle. Silent answered, the feller's hoss took lead which I'll have to admit was aimed for him, so he got behind its body 'n' forted up. Although young Thorny Bush, who you remember from when Waggles brought him into Child City, come up to see what was happening and wanted to chill the feller's milk some, Silent minded as I'd said I didn't want fuss and left him to get home afoot."

"Mind if I talk to this here Silent, if he don't live up to his name, and the young 'n'?" Reeves asked.

"I don't and Silent won't," Stone asserted with a grin, showing he had not taken offense at the suggestion. "'Specially if you should ask how he rescued a li'l ole Hereford bull calf from what he claims to be a whole slew of meat-eating critters who had it in mind to make a meal of it."

"Way you say that," the sheriff said, "I reckon I'll be smart to keep off *that* while we're talking. Then, after we've taken your lady's right kind invitation, you won't mind me going out to where it happened so as young Alvord can read the sign?"

"That's part of your job," Stone answered. "Which being, as a soon to be good taxpaying citizen of Spanish Grant County who likes to get value for my money, I'm all for the duly appointed and well-paid peace officers of said county doing plenty of work."

"Mind if I ask you to let your taxes let afore you start paying 'em?" the sheriff inquired with such a straight face that he, too, might have been in earnest. "There's already *way* too many with the same notion around."

"I was figuring on fetching the crew into town to celebrate finishing the drive soon," Stone remarked. "But I'll hold back on it until I've got your go-ahead."

"You've got it now, so don't forget to pay up your taxes with a smile," Reeves authorized in an amiable fashion. "Way your boy's've already been in behaved, 'specially Peaceful when he got pushed into what could have easy've wound up bad trouble, I don't figure they'll make any serious fuss even should any of the other crews happen by. They all got on good and friendly the first time, so everything's likely to stay as peaceable as Peaceful allows he just wants them to be."

---

1. *According to the story that was circulated and generally believed by cowhands, on being shown into the bunkhouse of a ranch newly taken over by John Chisum, the crew found its only furnishings to be a bottle of whisky in each corner. He makes guest appearances in* GOODNIGHT'S DREAM, FROM HIDE AND HORN, THE MAN FROM TEXAS, *and Part One,* "They Called Him the Cattle King," SLAUGHTER'S WAY.

11

NOBODY'S *TELLING* YOU
TO DO THAT

"You rode for the Union in the War of the Southern Secession, didn't you?" Jeremy Korbin asked, looking in a pointed fashion at the man he was addressing.

"Yes, sir," Amos Clitheroe replied with a touch of pride, despite his sole contribution to the federal side in the conflict having been as a member of the Quartermaster's Corps for the Union Army. "I had that honor."

The time was shortly before noon.

Despite the way in which he was speaking, the short, plump, and somewhat pompous owner of the only general store in Child City felt a trifle uneasy. Although his voice still retained its New England accent, he had spent enough time in towns west of the Mississippi River to be able to draw conclusions about the possible occupations of those with whom he came into contact. What he deduced about the two men who were the only other occupants of his premises gave him an uncomfortable feeling that came close to alarm. The sensation was all the stronger because he kept remembering that he had seen Sheriff Amon Reeves riding out of town accompanied by Deputy Burt Alvord about half an hour earlier and he had concluded from the mounts they had selected that they were expecting to cover a considerable distance before returning.

With the town's two tough and competent peace officers likely to be absent for an indefinite period, Clitheroe did not care for having a man whose attire might suggest he was a professional gambler but whose appearance implied he was also a fast gun come asking him such a question. Nor was he any better enamored of the cold-eyed, dangerous-looking hard case who was leaning in a faintly menacing fashion against the counter within reaching distance of a recently opened cracker-barrel.

"How do you feel about the new owner of the C Over M being a feller who was a captain in the *Confederate* Army?" Korbin inquired, reading something of the perturbation he and his companion were causing for the storekeeper and concluding that it could make what he had come to do easier.

"Well—!" Clitheroe began, instinct warning him that caution was required in the way he answered. "I haven't thought much about it."

"Then you'd best start thinking about it," Korbin stated, tapping his left forefinger on the top of the counter in a way that drew the attention of the storekeeper to it. "You see, there're some pretty good *customers* of your'n—and *one* in particular—who don't cotton to the notion of having a stinking Johnny Reb for a neighbor, nor to anybody as would deal with such trash."

"B-b—!" Clitheroe quavered. Having noticed that on the reference to "*one* in particular" the gambler's finger had traced a large AW on the counter, he drew a conclusion for which he had no liking. However, such was the comforting sense of security engendered by having the law enforced by

Sheriff Reeves that he was less worried than might have been the case in a less well-protected area. "But I can't refuse to do business with *anybody*."

"Nobody is *telling* you to do that," Korbin declared, wanting to be able to deny he had given any orders should the matter be reported to the local peace officer, a man he had heard would not be afraid to conduct an inquiry in response to the complaint. "Just make sure the Johnny Reb pays cash on the nail for everything he wants and don't be overeager to get him anything you haven't got to hand. You'll find there'll be plenty of folks—" At which point his finger once again made the AW. "All of who spend a fair bit of money regularly with you, who'll think high of you for doing it."

"There's something else for you to think on," the burly hard case put in, forgetting the instructions he had been given and, having no liking for the way in which his companion acted as if everybody else were of secondary importance, feeling he would make his presence felt more than he had so far since entering the store. "*Accidents* happen to them as don't take notice real good of what they get telled."

" *'Accidents'?*" Clitheroe repeated with a similar emphasis on the word, although the timbre was more perturbed than menacing. Seeing the speaker take out a box of matches and strike one, he went on worriedly, "How do you mean, *accidents*?"

"Well, like say somebody getting so all-fired careless he dropped a lit match in this here cracker barrel," the hard case elaborated. "I bet they'd flare up real good, and any as wasn't burned couldn't be sold."

"I—I—!" Clitheroe gasped, realizing that the last part of what he had heard was the truth.

"Give me a light afore you blow it out," Korbin commanded, extracting a cigar from his vest pocket and eyeing

his companion in a cold manner. When this was done in a
more grudging fashion than such a request should have
elicited, he returned his gaze to Clitheroe and his free forefinger traced another AW on the top of the counter. "Just
you keep in mind what I've told you, Mr. Clitheroe, and
nobody will think any the worse of you."

"I—I'll bear it in mind," the storekeeper promised.

"From now on, leave the talking to me!" Korbin growled
as he and his companion walked along the wheel-rutted
street toward the next business upon which they were going
to call.

"I figured to throw a scare into him," the hard case replied sullenly.

"Just leave all the figuring to *me*," the gambler commanded. "I told you that I want to be able to say there
wasn't nothing threatening said should the great seizer
come asking."

"He's already rid out to see the beefheads about what
Skinny told him," the hard case reminded, having no liking
for the first part of what had just been said to him.

"And he'll be back when he gets to know the rights of
what did happen, which he will easy enough with the
damned 'breed Alvord along to read the sign," Korbin answered coldly. "Don't forget, he's no Wyatt Earp to be
ready to take anything he gets told about a Texan cattleman
as being the truth. He'll listen to their side and check what
he's seen. Then he'll come back and somebody could tell
him what we've been doing."

"He got you scared?" the hard case sneered.

"*Nobody's* got me scared," the gambler stated flatly. "Or
do *you* reckon there could be an exception around here?"

"Naw," the hard case denied, sensing that circumstances
were not sufficiently in his favor for him to take up what
had clearly been a challenge directed his way.

"That's *good*," Korbin declared. Satisfied that he still

maintained his moral ascendancy over the other man, he decided to amplify his reason for adopting such a stance. "I'm not scared of Reeves, but I want it to look like it's *him* at fault should we have to lock horns. Now let's get on with what we've come to do."

"Why aren't we going to do it at the State?" the hard case inquired, nodding toward the saloon at the other side of the street.

"That's being handled by somebody else," the gambler replied with a mocking sneer playing on his lips that suggested he felt the task would not be the kind of success he could have produced. "So I've been told we've got to stay clear to leave it to them."

* * *

"There's one coming now!"

Possibly because the time was shortly after noon, very little business was being done in the barroom of the Arizona State Saloon.

Only half a dozen customers were present, and each was holding nothing more than a partially empty glass of beer. Four were seated at a table in the center and one of the remaining pair stood looking out of a front window. Although none had gunbelts or visible weapons, their attire—grubby and untidy—was that of working cowhands. However, to anybody with experience of men in cattle-raising country, there were suggestions that none earned a living from such employment. Their badly shaved and generally unprepossessing faces were all sun-reddened rather than tanned from long hours in the open air. In fact, the voice of the man by the right-side window who had drawn the attention of the seated group by speaking had the accent of an Easterner—and one with some education at that.

Although Peter Medak had not been in range country a long time, he did not believe the customers were cowhands. In fact, he was aware of why they were loafing around the barroom. As he had been told would prove the case when receiving his orders from the man in the alley, their purpose would provide him with just enough sales—along with grudgingly supplied gratuities, which he had already demanded and would never disclose to his employer, who had expressed surprise when he volunteered to take the morning shift—to present him with the semblance of doing enough business to justify opening early.

Hearing the announcement made by Alastair Beaton, the rest of the customers and the sullen-faced bartender waited to see what kind of man they would be dealing with if he should be there for the purpose they had been sent to prevent. At the batwing doors being opened and him entering, none of the occupants of the barroom found him an impressive sight.

Even aided by his high-heeled tan-colored boots, the newcomer was no more than five feet six in height. Neatly trimmed dusty blond hair showed from beneath the wide brim of his black, low-crowned, Texas-style J. B. Stetson hat. Not much beyond his early twenties, he was moderately good-looking, but there was nothing particularly eye-catching about his tanned and clean-shaven face when it was in repose. The tightly rolled scarlet silk bandanna, dark green shirt, and Levi's pants he was wearing had been purchased recently, but he contrived to give them the appearance of being somebody else's castoffs and they tended to emphasize rather than conceal his small stature. Nor, despite the rig having been made by a master craftsman, was his appearance made more impressive by his wearing a well-designed brown gunbelt with twin bone-handled Colt 1873 Model Peacemaker revolvers butt forward for a cross-draw in its contoured holsters. Nevertheless, if one took the trouble to look closely, there was a strength of will and intelligence about his features, and his muscular development was that of a Hercules in miniature.

Neither the bartender nor the customers took the trouble to look closely, so they accepted the newcomer at face value.

"Howdy, sir," the cowhand greeted, crossing to the counter and directing the words to the fat bartender. Not unexpectedly, considering the way he was dressed, his voice was that of a Texan. While speaking, he shoved back his Stetson so it dangled by its *barbiquejo* chin strap on his shoulders. "Could you tell me how I'd find the Wedge—no, you'll likely still know it as the C Over M—spread?"

"Hey, you!" James Scroggie, the tallest of the seated group, put in before any reply could be given. Rising, he walked forward accompanied by Brian Gould, who was the next in height. "Don't you know it's against the law to walk around wearing guns in Child City?"

"Well, no, sir," the dusty-blond replied, turning toward the speaker. "I can't truthful true say as I'd heard tell of such a thing."

"Well, it is," Scroggie stated. "And you'd best take them off right now."

"Would you be a peace officer, sir?" the small Texan inquired mildly.

"No!" Scroggie denied vehemently. He had the kind of mentality that saw any and everything concerned with law and order as repugnant, so he resented its being suggested that he might be thought one of its minions. "But it's still the law here in Child City."

"Well, such being so," the dusty-blond drawled, starting to release the pigging thongs attaching the bottoms of the holsters to his thighs as a prelude to removing the gunbelt.

"I'm really pleased to meet somebody with such a respect for the law," Scroggie said after having thrown a quick glance at his seated companions while the Texan was placing the rig on the counter of the bar. Extending his right hand, he went on, "Shake, friend."

The offer was accepted, but instead of merely shaking the hand he took, Scroggie began to squeeze. Before he could increase the pressure and deliver a warning that the cowhand must not go to the C Over M ranch, a strange and alarming metamorphosis seemed to take place. Suddenly the cowhand no longer gave the impression of being small and insignificant, but appeared to take on size and bulk until he loomed larger than anybody else present. Under less trying conditions, Scroggie might have seen that it was merely the strength of the Texan's personality that wrought the change. At that moment, however, he was conscious only of feeling his own fingers being gripped with a strength that—along with the uncanny alteration to his intended victim's hitherto innocuous aspect—took him completely by surprise. Nor was that the end of his misfortune. Suddenly his hand was twisted palm upward so that the wrist was bent in an even more painful fashion.

Realizing that something had gone very wrong with a system that had yielded good results in the past, Gould took a pace forward. Also arriving at the same conclusion, David Finch and Allen Yentob came to their feet at the table. Although equally taken aback by the unexpected way in which the situation at the bar was developing, Beaton and Douglas McAvoy decided that the rest of their party could cope with it and remained by their respective windows. However, having little faith in their ability where anything requiring courage or fighting skill was concerned and being mindful that the gunbelt was in easy reaching distance of the small Texan, Medak reached for the wooden bung-starter that was kept on the shelf behind the counter and that served the dual purpose of beer-barrel opener and extemporized weapon in the event of trouble.

Without relaxing the grip he was exerting on Scroggie's hand, the small Texan responded to the approach with a similar speed, and even more effectively. Rising rapidly, the sharp toe of his left boot took Gould full between the legs. Caught on such a susceptible portion of his anatomy, Gould let out a gurgling croak and, folding over with hands clasped at the point of impact, stumbled away a few steps before collapsing to his knees.

Seeing that the situation was going in an unsatisfactory fashion, Medak lifted the bung-starter to change things in favor of the men with whom he was working. However, in his haste, he inadvertently caused a slight clatter while doing so. Hearing and forming the correct conclusion of what the sound portended, the small Texan continued to react quickly. Aided by the painful hold on Scroggie's wrist, the blond caused him to swing around until it was he who stood with his back to the bar.. Unable to prevent his motion, Medak brought the bung-starter down on the wrong head. Although Scroggie was wearing a hat, it was a cheap "woolsey" no self-respecting cowhand would have deigned to own; a J. B. Stetson might have fended off the impact to a greater extent. The blow rendered Scroggie unconscious.

As Scroggie crumpled, the cowhand transferred his left hand to the back of the bartender's close-cropped head and slammed his face on the top of the counter in a most painful fashion. Set free the moment the impact took effect, his assailant's attention being diverted elsewhere, Scroggie lurched backward blinded by pain and with blood gushing from a broken nose. He collided against the wall, bringing a couple of bottles toppling from the shelves, and rebounded against the counter. The force of his arrival was enough to make the gunbelt fall, and he crumpled to his knees with hands clasped to his face.

Alert to everything else that was happening while dealing with Medak, the small Texan saw Finch and Yentob advance in a threatening fashion, clearly intending to take revenge for what had happened to their companions. Without waiting to make sure he had rendered the bartender *hors de combat,* he placed both palms on the counter as an aid to hoisting himself up to sit on it. The smallest of his party, Yentob had allowed Finch to take the lead, and he now saw he had made a wise decision. Alighting on the bar counter the blond swung up his left leg before the nearer of the approaching men could lay hands on him, or even realize the danger.

Rising beneath Finch's jaw, the kick that was delivered proved as efficacious as the one that had left Gould writhing in agony and retching on the floor. As his companion was going down, Yentob, deciding that the situation was getting far too dangerous for him, tried to halt his own advance. His hopes along that line proved of no avail. The small Texan thrust himself from the counter and alighted within striking distance of Yentob. The backhand slap that caught Yentob on the cheek sent him sprawling to his hands and knees farther along the bar.

Having watched what was happening with a growing sense of mingled amazement and alarm, Beaton and McAvoy concluded that dealing with such a competent bare-handed fighter demanded sterner measures than anyone had employed thus far. With that in mind, each of them reached for the revolver he had concealed beneath the jacket he was wearing. They were confident they could draw and use the weapons before the small Texan could retrieve the guns that had fallen with his gunbelt from the bar.

12

HE ATTACKED US WITHOUT THE SLIGHTEST PROVOCATION

Even as the two members of the group who had been instructed to wait at the Arizona State Saloon and deter any cowhands from going to seek work at the C Over M ranch—by which name it was still known in Child City—were preparing to take action, there was an interruption to their plans.

With the screech of metal being dragged from wood, the right side of the batwing doors was torn from the jamb and a young man came through with it in his grasp. The man responsible for the damage would stand out in any company. Looking even taller than his six-foot-three height, with golden-blond hair and almost classically handsome tanned features showing intelligence and strength of will, he was a magnificent physical specimen. He had a great spread to his shoulders and he tapered to a narrow waist that opened out onto long legs ending in high-heeled, sharp-toed cowhand boots. His clothes were those of a range-country dandy but they were clearly functional and had been worn for work. He wore a Texas-style white J. B. Stetson—its crown encircled by a well-polished black leather band bearing silver *conchas*—and a tightly rolled blue silk bandanna trailing its long ends down his broad chest. The dark blue shirt and Levi's he had on were clearly made to his measure; such an excellent fit for one of his size could not have come off the shelves of a store. Clearly made by a master craftsman, his brown leather *buscadero* gunbelt carried two ivory-handled Colt Cavalry Model Peacemakers in contoured holsters designed to permit their very rapid withdrawal by anyone with the necessary skill.

Instead of reaching for his weapons as he swung toward Alastair Beaton, the blond giant proved that his considerable heft did not render him slow-moving or clumsy. Swung with no greater difficulty than was displayed during its removal, the door was hurled with such good aim that it struck the surly-faced young Easterner and swept him from his feet. The short-barreled Merwin & Hulbert Army pocket revolver the Easterner had taken out with the intention of using on the small Texan by the bar fell from his grasp.

Nor did Douglas McAvoy fare any better in dealing with the insignificant-looking dusty-blond cowhand.

An instant after the big dandy-dresser had made his spectacular entrance, another man, just as obviously Texan, followed in a less dramatic but no slower fashion.

Three inches shorter than his companion, the other newcomer was lean as a steer raised in greasewood country and exuded a boundless, whipcord strength. What could be seen of his hair was as black as the wing of a deep-South crow. Indian dark, his good-looking face had lines of what would have suggested a babyish innocence had it not been for his curious red-hazel eyes. With the exception of the dark brown walnut grips of an old Colt First Model Dragoon revolver, turned forward for a low cavalry twist-hand draw in the holster on the right side of his gunbelt, and the ivory hilt of a massive James Black bowie knife at its left, every item he wore—the boots having heels more suited to walking than riding—was black. In addition to his other armament, he carried a magnificent Winchester Model of 1873 rifle with the casual ease of one long used to doing so.

"Let it drop, *hombre!*" commanded the black-clad Texan, his voice a pleasant tenor that nevertheless had a hard and somehow chillingly savage note.

Turning as he heard the words, McAvoy, shortest of the group and thickset, gave no indication of being willing to comply. He was filled with the hatred all of his kind had for Southrons, and was long noted for refusing to conform unquestioningly to the "liberal" ideals that he and all his companions—the bartender to an even more radical degree—possessed. His decision was also induced by a fear of what might happen if he did yield and discard his British-made Webley Bulldog revolver, as well as by a spurious sense of courage produced by the marijuana in the cigarette he was smoking.

Before McAvoy could turn his snub-nosed weapon into a new alignment, he saw the black-dressed Texan move his way with a speed too rapid for his dulled mind to respond in any positive way. All the seeming innocence had left the other's handsome face, to be replaced by a savage mask that reminded him of paintings he had seen purporting to show Indians charging to the attack. Coming around with a sweeping motion of the Texan's right arm, which was clearly endowed with powerful muscles to be able to handle the nine-and-a-half-pound weight of the Winchester with such ease, the twenty-six-inch-long octagonal barrel slammed against the side of the stocky Easterner's head. Bright lights seemed to erupt inside the Easterner's head as he went staggering, but blackness descended before he struck the wall and bounced off to sprawl without movement on the floor.

As any member of the regular Wedge crew and numerous other people throughout the West could have told McAvoy, he was very fortunate to have come out of the affair alive. Nothing in the birthright and upbringing of the Ysabel Kid had been calculated to imbue him with an overstrong sense of the sanctity of human life.[1] There had been a time a few years ago when, had he come across the scene that greeted him and Mark Counter as they were about to follow Dusty Fog into the saloon—after having halted at the leather worker's store next door to ask one another why cowhands in Arizona did not adopt a double-girthed rig such as that all Texans used—he would not have hesitated before dealing with McAvoy in a fatal fashion.

"Dad-blast it, Dusty," the Kid growled as he and the blond giant started to walk forward. "Can't you go no place without getting into a fuss?"

"I declare he's getting worse than Red Blaze for so doing,"[2] Mark asserted in a baritone Texas drawl suggestive of his having received a better formal education than his black-dressed *amigo* had.[3] "Why, he couldn't even keep clear of trouble when we split up that time to see who could reach Tensonville over to New Mexico without getting into any on the way."

"That he couldn't," the Kid agreed. "Then he got all sneaky 'n' allowed he'd won the blasted bet 'cause he'd reached Tensonville afore he got into any, even though he was hip-deep with the water over the willows in it when we rode in to pull his chestnuts offen the stovetop."[4]

"What set it off *this* time?" the blond giant inquired, watching his small companion retrieve and start to strap on the gunbelt.

Before Dusty Fog could reply, the door behind the bar opened and the owner of the saloon came in.[5] He was of medium height, with a stout build and choleric features that concealed a warm and generous nature, as did his pretense at being a dour and penny-pinching Highland Scot, an effect he augmented by always wearing a woollen bonnet surmounted by a pompom and trews in the tartan coloring of his clan. Angus McTavish did not lack courage. No man would have dared adopt such a form of headdress in a range-country town if he did. On seeing Medak sprawled bloody and barely conscious on the floor behind the bar along with two broken bottles of his stock, he swung his gaze quickly to the other side of the counter. His sense of puzzlement was increased with each separate thing that came to his view.

"What the devil—?" the owner began in his pronounced Scottish burr as his right hand went under the left side of his lightweight off-white jacket.

"Wouldn't do that, was I you, mister," the Kid warned in what was a mild tone. But although the Kid was resting the barrel of his Winchester pointed backward over his right shoulder, the man to whom the words were directed did not regard them in such a light.

"Not unless you're in cahoots with this bunch of knobheads and want to take it up for them," Mark supplemented. Although his hands hung clear of the ivory butts of his twin Colts, his bearing struck the Scot as being equally menacing.

"I own this place, I'll have to admit," McTavish announced. "But I don't know what you mean by being in cahoots with them. The only one I know is my barkeep, who's lying back here."

"Do tell," Dusty drawled, having replaced his gunbelt. However, he too made no hostile gestures as he continued in a matter-of-fact tone, "If he acts like he tried to with me against your other customers, he must lose you a heap of them."

"You maybe better be telling me what it's all about, Cap'n Fog," McTavish requested, recognizing the full potential of the small Texan and recalling where he had last been seen.

"He attacked us without the slightest provocation," Allen Yentob squawked in an effeminate-sounding New England accent, shaking his head in an attempt to clear it of the dizziness caused by the backhand blow it had received.

"What, *all* of you at once?" the Kid scoffed. "Dusty, you're certain sure getting worse'n good ole Red ever was."

"Way Dusty goes busting into fuss head down and horns a-hooking regardless these days, Mr. Saloonkeeper," Mark commented. "This no-bullfighter *could* be telling the truthful true of it, *amigo*."

"And if cows could fly and they'd been drinking croton oil, we'd sure need to go 'round wearing our slickers while they was overhead," the black-dressed Texan countered. "Which, afore anybody tells me, I'm danged uncouth."

"How long've you known a six-dollar word like uncouth?" Dusty queried.

"Ever since your sweet li'l cousin Betty said I was it," the Kid answered. "Which, the way she looked and sounded, I sort of got to figuring it wasn't *nice*."[6]

"I reckon we'd better have the sheriff in here," McTavish stated, contriving with an effort to prevent himself from showing how amusing he had found the interplay between the Texans. "Unless you'd sooner not, Cap'n Fog?"

"I'm all for it," the small Texan answered without hesitation. "There's your barkeep and the jasper he whomped on the head with a bung-starter to think on. They and maybe a couple more could use a doctor."

"I'll send for 'em both," the saloonkeeper offered. Then his eyes went to the front entrance, which he had not noticed while looking at the rest of the room. "Hey, what happened to my door?"

"It sort of come off in my hand," Mark replied. "And I got so carried away when I saw that *hombre* it's lying on throw down on Dusty, when Dusty wasn't wearing his guns to do anything about it, I just natural' threw it at him."

"And so would *anybody* in the same circumstances," McTavish asserted, although he realized that there were few men who could have duplicated either tearing free the side of the door or throwing it with the force that must have been used.

"I'll pay to have it fixed on again," the blond giant offered.

"Let's wait and see who Amon Reeves, same being our sheriff, figures should be doing the paying, shall we?" the saloonkeeper said, then ran an unfriendly gaze over the frightened young New Englander. "Seeing as they're all your friends, looks like, you'd best go fetch the both of them to us."

"Th-this is the first time I've been here," Yentob yelled in a voice that sounded close to tears. "I don't know where to find either of them."

At that moment, the door behind the bar was opened again and another of the bartenders came through it.

"Just dropped by for a be—!" the man started. Then he stared about him with eyes bugging and showing even more reaction to the sight than his employer had. "What's come off here, boss?"

"You can hear all about it when you've fetched the sheriff 'n' Doc Gottlinger," McTavish replied, noticing without any undue surprise that no consideration was being shown for the condition to which Medak—never having been popular with the rest of the staff—had been reduced. "It'll save a muckle amount of time, which is money, I've always been told, and having it told twice."

"I can get Doc easy enough, boss," the bartender declared, amused as always by his employer's pretense of being devoted to the saving of money by any means. "Only, I saw Amon and young Alvord riding by my place a bit back, and he allowed he'd got to be away on some lawman's chore that'd take a fair while, was anybody to ask me."

                              *   *   *

"Those of them the doctor could get talking stuck to it that Scroggie was only fixing to have some of the fun they'd read about us cowhands having when he started to squeeze at my hand," Dusty Fog told Stone Hart as they stood together at the bar of the Arizona State Saloon. "And the rest of them cut in because they reckoned I was playing too rough for it to be taken as a joke. The barkeep claimed it had always been his training to support the regular customers again' a stranger."

All around the two Texans, acknowledged as the leaders of their respective outfits, the crew of the Wedge mingled with Mark Counter and The Ysabel Kid—who were held in esteem surmounted only by that accorded to Dusty and Stone—to celebrate within the bounds of behavior they had been told would be considered acceptable. For their part, the boss of the Wedge and the *segundo* of the OD Connected were discussing the events of the day before joining in the festivities.

Stone had started by telling about the visit from Sheriff Amon Reeves, explaining that the examination of the sign by Deputy Burt Alvord—with Kiowa Cotton invited at the senior peace officer's request to act in the capacity of an expert witness where such matters were concerned—at the scene of the shooting had proved that Silent Churchman had spoken the truth about what took place. Not only had the two lawmen accompanied the Wedge into Child City, but Reeves had insisted that Margaret Hart—who had left behind her dog so as to avoid drawing any more attention to her blindness than was necessary—and Steffie Willis stay as guests of his wife after concluding their business in Child

City. Furthermore, delighted to make two new acquaintances, Becky Reeves had acted as guide for the two women while they were doing their chores.

"But they allowed they were only in town for the first time today," Stone pointed out.

"That's what Amon Reeves reminded the jasper who said it," Dusty replied. "So the barkeep said as how they'd been good paying customers ever since he opened and he knew how cowhands tended to treat dudes mean, so figured it was up to him to stop me doing it."

"All of them and just the one of you, 'n' you having put your guns on the bar afore it started," the boss of the Wedge said in tones of derision, having had the events that took place at the saloon recounted at the conclusion of his own explanation. "Where you reckon they'd come from?"

"Allowed to be staying as paying guests on one of the local ranches."

"Which one?"

"They got sort of edgy about that, saying they didn't want word of what had happened getting back, as they might be told to light a shuck for home," Dusty replied. "But Amon—who strikes me like you as a good, fair, and smart lawman—made them spit it out. They reckoned it was with the new boss of what used to be—"

"The L Scissors, only it's been changed to the AW."

"Sounds like you know the gent concerned," Dusty remarked.

"We've never so much as laid eyes on one another, so far as I know," Stone replied. "But I'm starting to get the feeling it's only going to be a matter of time before we have to get 'round to it. According to what that gunny, Korbin, allowed it was him who sent them to cut our herd, and there's been hints that he's done more'n just that since it happened."

"He doesn't sound any too friendly, Stone," the small

Texan remarked. "If you've never met, do you have any notion why?"

"All I can figure," the boss of the Wedge answered, "him having been a major with the New Jersey Dragoons in Arkansas when you and the rest of Ole Devil's bunch were running the Yankees ragged, he's still wanting to keep the War going again' us Johnny Rebs whether we served there or not. Hell, *amigo*, what with having Margaret along and all, the last thing I want is for fuss starting hereabouts, 'specially over something like that."

1. *Information about the background and upbringing of the Ysabel Kid is given in Appendix Three.*
2. *Information about Red Blaze and his penchant for frequently becoming embroiled in fights is to be found in various volumes of the Civil War and Floating Outfit series.*
3. *Details concerning the family background and special qualifications of Mark Counter are to be found in Appendix Two.*
4. *The events being discussed in the conversation are described in* THE TEXAN.
5. *The pertinent details pertaining to Dusty Fog are given in Appendix One.*
6. *The exact relationship between General Ole Devil Hardin and his "granddaughter," Elizabeth, "Betty," is a matter upon which the members of the clan from whom we receive the information to produce many of our books will make no comment. Accounts of some of her adventures are recorded in various volumes in the Civil War and Floating Outfit series. She "stars" in her own account for* Part Four, "It's Our Turn To Improvise, Miss Blaze," *J.T.'s* LADIES, GUNSMOKE THUNDER, *and* TEXAS KIDNAPPERS.

13
THAT MAKES *THREE* OF THEM!

"Not long afore I was good enough to let Cap'n Hart have my invaluable services, my uncle, who was an undertaker, died." Thorny Bush stated gravely. Holding a schooner of beer and hoping he looked as if doing so was an everyday event in his life, he was standing in front of the Ysabel Kid at the Arizona State Saloon, at the end of the bar opposite to where his boss and Dusty Fog were concluding their discussion. "Comes the will-reading time, which all the family goes to natural', families being what they are, turns out he left the whole shebang to my cousin Zeb. Well, Daddy says to Cousin Zeb, 'Are you going to take it on?' 'n' Cousin Zeb says right back, 'Why, sure, I've done got me my first customer'!"

"Sounds like your cousin Zeb was a real slick *hombre*," the black-dressed Texan drawled soberly, his Indian-dark face giving no indication that he was enjoying the account. However, he continued, "So did said Cousin Zeb make a go of his undertakering?"

"Had a mite of trouble at his first funeral," Bush claimed, delighted to have found a fresh and apparently receptive audience for the jokes he had been telling on numerous occasions since joining the Wedge crew and starting the drive. "The corpse got throwed out of the back of the hearse, and you'll *never* guess where they found it."

"Which being, I won't even *try,*" the Kid declared, noticing that Silent Churchman, Dude, and some of the other temporary Wedge hands were gathering behind the youngster. "Where did they find him, or her, whichever said corpse might be?"

"In the doctor's," Bush replied. "It was saying, 'Have you got anything to stop me coffin'!"

"That does it!" the stocky Wedge hand bawled at the top of his voice. "Let's send him to find some place where he'll be 'preciated, which he sure's hell *ain't* in here!"

Giving the youngster no time to even realize what was coming, much less resist, Silent and Dude grabbed him by the arms. A moment later, the Welsh cowhand, David Montgomerie, and one of the others caught hold of his ankles. Lifting him with the deft skill acquired by helping to throw and hold down cattle of various sizes for branding during a roundup, they kept their holds as, Bush's body bucking and writhing in futile attempts to get free, he was carried to the front entrance.

Bush also cut loose with a flow of blistering profanity that caused Dusty Fog to remark to Stone Hart—as they watched what was happening with amused tolerance—that he must have been receiving instruction in more than just working on a trail drive from Silent and Peaceful Gunn. In fact, the small Texan said he figured that Chow Willicka must have added to his vocabulary as well. For his part, having joined the two bosses on seeing they had concluded their business, Mark Counter said he felt sure the youngster must have made an extensive and more than platonic acquaintance with Calamity Jane, whose repertoire along those lines he had good reason to know.[1] There was considerable encouragement being given to the extemporized bearer party. Even the garishly dressed and not too bad-looking young women hired by Angus McTavish to offer female company for the customers were joining in the clamor and showing no sign of being offended by the copious flow of bad language from the victim.

However, neither the struggles by the youngster nor the invective were to any avail. The batwing door that Mark Counter had ripped off to throw at Alastair Beaton had been replaced, but it proved to pose no obstacle for Bush's captors. He was carried across the sidewalk and dumped unceremoniously in the dust at the center of the street. With this done, Silent informed him that they had put him where he belonged, and his assailants trooped back into the saloon.

"Blast those no-account wall-eyed, spavined bunch of hard-winterers!" Bush declaimed, but there was neither malice nor annoyance in his voice. Without realizing he was speaking aloud, he came to his feet and instinctively began knocking the dust from his "go-to-town" clothes. Remembering what he had been taught from his early childhood, he had halted the obscenities on finding himself being removed from the saloon to where there might be "good" women present. "I'll pay 'em all back, see if I don't."

Wondering how he could bring about his threat to the best advantage, the youngster heard a snicker redolent of mocking amusement from his rear. Thinking it must be originating from one of his tormentors, he elected to ignore it. Then the sound turned to a bitter and unfriendly laugh.

Despite his professed Scottish reluctance to waste money on nonessentials, McTavish maintained enough lamps outside to illuminate the front of the saloon in a most adequate fashion. Because of the lighting, Bush, wheeling in

the direction from which the derisive sound came, was able
to see a figure he recognized coming around the corner of
the building. There was a mocking leer on the face of the
man whose horse had been shot from under him by Silent
during the gathering of C Over M cattle for rebranding.
What was more, his right hand was suspended by its thumb
over his gunbelt, close to the butt of the off-side Colt.

The youngster knew that such a posture of readiness was
sometimes adopted when trouble was expected, or the one
behaving in such a fashion was ready and eager to start
some.

"Do the other beefhead bastards pick on you regular,
sonny?" Skinny McBride asked in a voice devoid of all
humor.

Bearing in mind his boss's strict instructions against becoming involved in trouble during the visit to town, although his lips compressed to a thin line white against the
tan of his face, Bush forced himself to continue the dusting-
off process without offering any reply.

But the scrawny man was not to be put off by the lack of
response.

The additional mockery to which McBride had been
subjected after having returned on foot from his self-
appointed mission of vengeance had added to the hatred
he had developed for the Texans, especially the one he
regarded as being responsible for his latest fall from grace.
Nor had he been enamored of the orders he had recently
received. Although the other four and a half-breed who
had remained behind during the abortive attempt to cut the
Wedge herd were going to carry out a scheme thought up
by Jeremy Korbin, he had been told curtly to return to the
ranch where they were staying as soon as he had seen Sheriff Amon Reeves leave accompanied by Deputy Alvord to
investigate his supposed complaint about the incident resulting in the loss of his horse. Instead of following the

instructions, and despite knowing they were a precaution against his being questioned for lying about what took place when the lawmen returned, he had spent the time until nightfall at the small "house of ill repute" that operated in the partial concealment offered by a grove of trees.

From what McBride had been told by one of the prostitutes, most of the Wedge crew had arrived in Child City toward sundown. Hoping to find an opportunity to take revenge on the stocky cowhand who had shot his mount, he had decided to do so by firing into the barroom from the sidewalk and then making good his escape on the horse he had left tethered at the rear of the saloon. With that in mind, he had passed along the alley separating it from the next building.

Peering around the corner, the scrawny hard case had seen the eviction of the youngster from the saloon. The main object of his spleen was among one of the quartet doing the carrying, but—imbued with a strong streak of caution—he had felt disinclined to press his advantage at the moment: as soon as he fired, the other three Texans would be well-placed to take action. Instead, he saw a far safer course of action, even though it would have a detrimental effect upon his main ambition.

Thinking fast, the hard case told himself that killing the youngster would provoke a hunt that might offer an opportunity to pick off the stocky cowhand. But there was an even more important point than the possibility of achieving his vengeance to take into account. He was not disinclined to commit murder, but as there was a chance that somebody might see what happened—although he saw no possible witnesses along the street and most of the nearest business places were already closed for the night—he felt it advisable to kill the youngster in what could be regarded as a fair fight. He did not think that doing so would be hard to achieve regardless of how the other was armed. Not only did he believe that the two Colts worn by his intended victim were merely an attempt to create a sense of toughness, but he felt he knew enough about cowhands in town for a celebration to be confident that the other had already taken enough drinks to make himself an easy mark.

"I've heard tell folks sometimes make glue from dead hosses," Bush countered, goaded into replying by the derogatory reference to men from his home state. "And conclude *you'd* maybe know something about that!"

"I said I've heard tell as how all you goddamned beefheads like picking on fellers littler'n themselves 'cause it's easier 'n' safer'n trying to take on somebody their own size," the hard case snarled. He continued to be provocatively insulting, since he was determined to provoke the youngster into a move that could be considered hostile. "Do they get at *you* regular on account of that?"

"Oh, just about as often as *you* lose a hoss, I reckon," the youngster countered.

"You talk *real* big for a wet-behind-the-ears beefhead button who reckons he's a man growed," McBride asserted, the memory of the loss of his horse and the long walk back to where he had left his companions still rankling enough to make him want to force the issue. "How's about seeing if you can act like one?"

"Anytime you want to give it a whirl at finding out," Bush found himself answering before he fully appreciated the consequences, "make your play!"

"Don't you draw on me!" the hard case snapped, trying to pitch his voice at a level that would be heard by anybody on the street but not by the occupants of the saloon.

Having supplied what he thought sufficient inducement for the response he required, and despite his assertion about the lack of ability his opponent would show, McBride had no intention of leaving it to chance. He sent his right hand to close about the butt of his Colt Peacemaker so as to bring it from the holster. He was completely confident of success and was already planning how he would make his escape when he had achieved his purpose. Regardless of all he had done to give a spurious justification for his behavior, he had no intention of allowing any of the Texans in the saloon to be the ones to whom he would explain it. Knowing how he would react to such a situation, he did not doubt that they would be just as quick to do the same and that he would be subjected to fatal summary justice on the spot.

With a feeling of something close to alarm, Bush realized that he was involved in a life-or-death situation. Fortunately for him, however, he did not allow this feeling to numb him into a condition of inactivity. Rather, he behaved with a coolness he would later view as remarkable. What was more, despite the urgency of the situation, he did not forget the advice he had received since becoming accepted as a member of the Wedge trail crew.

Having taken a liking to the spunky youngster when satisfied he would make a hand, Dude, like the rest of the men on the trail drive, had decided to steer him in the right direction where one aspect was concerned. While he would not class himself anywhere close to Dusty Fog and Mark Counter in matters *pistolero,* the dandy dresser considered himself competent enough to be able to proffer sound advice. Therefore, with the consent he had requested being granted by Stone Hart, he had set about passing on the wisdom he had acquired over the years, and he found he had a ready pupil with a natural flair for gun handling.

At this, the first moment of serious trial in his young life, Bush put to use without conscious thought what was probably the best of the advice given by Dude. From the beginning he had been taught that, although he was wearing the two ivory-handled Colt Civilian Model Peacemakers in the same manner he had heard attributed to his hero, Captain Dusty Fog, very few men could duplicate the handling of the weapons with the facility displayed by the Rio Hondo gun wizard. Therefore, at Dude's instigation—and the rest of the crew's approval—he had concentrated on drawing the left-side weapon while retaining its mate for use in case more than six shots should be required in an emergency.

McBride drew his gun at the best speed he could achieve. But, his gunbelt not being of a quality that would allow the rapidity a top hand in such matters could attain, he was assailed by a sudden and sickening realization that things were not going the way he had expected. Until that moment, he had been convinced he was dealing with nothing more than a dressed-up and probably part-drunk kid who would prove easy meat. That his intended victim had not displayed any of the signs that he had been on the liquor prior to being evicted from the saloon had failed to strike the hard case until too late.

With the speed he had acquired as the result of practice taken during the drive, even though later he could not remember having consciously given himself the order to do so, the youngster's right hand closed on the butt of the left-side Colt. At that moment, the insistence of his father on purchasing a well-designed rig to carry his weapons paid its dividend. Sliding free and turning outward almost of its own volition, it seemed to its owner, the revolver was placed at waist level and in instinctive alignment on his tormentor. However, having brought this about, Bush hesitated before completing the movement.

The hesitation almost cost the youngster his life.

Granted the opportunity, and although he realized he had been beaten to the draw, McBride got off a shot.

However, in his state of alarm, the hard case failed to make a hit.

Refusing to be deterred or thrown into a panic by hearing for the first time the sound of lead whizzing by very close to his head, Bush reacted instinctively. The Colt roared and bucked in his hand. Although he was momentarily dazzled by the sudden glare resulting from the lead being emitted, he sensed that he had made a hit. Nor were his faculties at fault. Flying as directed by his subconscious instructions, the .45 bullet took his tormentor in the left breast. Flung backward with his own weapon flying from his suddenly inoperative grasp, the hard case went down in an untidy sprawl to the street.

The shots were heard inside the saloon, and all thoughts of celebrating immediately left the heads of the Texans, although the same did not apply to the three members of Ole Devil's floating outfit. The Texans were certain the youngster would not have forgotten the instructions given by their boss and fired off his gun in the street as a way of avenging himself for the way he was treated. Therefore, headed by Dusty and Stone, there was a concerted rush for the front door. After emerging from the saloon, they found Bush standing with his Colt dangling by his side and a look of dawning realization coming to his face.

"I—He—I—!" the youngster gasped, turning toward his boss and other hero.

"We *know,* boy," Stone said gently, then swung around to look at the others who were coming out of the barroom. "It's over, boys, go back to your funning."

"Sure, boss," Waggles Harrison assented, realizing why the order had been given and wanting to help grant the time Bush needed to recover from what he knew must be serious concern over what had happened. "Come on, fellers, Silent's promised *not* to tell us how he saved his pride 'n' joy from all them swarms of mean critters' as was fixing to eat it."

"Sheriff's coming," the Kid drawled in a laconic fashion before Stone could speak with the clearly shaken youngster, he and Mark having remained on the street while the rest were returning.

"What happened?" Reeves inquired on arriving. He had been making his usual rounds of the town when he had heard the shooting.

"H-he come up and start bad-mouthing me," Bush replied, taking comfort from seeing his boss standing supportively by his side. "We drew and—!"

"Looks to me like a case of slow," the Kid suggested as Bush's explanation came to an end. "Why'd he come after you, boy—? Sorry, Sheriff, I know it's you as should be doing the asking."

"I thought all you Injuns was the strong 'n' silent kind," Reeves declared, showing he felt no resentment over the usurping of his duty. Gesturing toward the body, he went on, "This is the feller who came in with the complaint about Silent, Stone. I was wanting to meet up with him and ask why-for he told me such a pack of lies. Well, looks like I'll never get the chance. Looks like he was hunting for evens over losing his hoss and picked on you 'cause Silent wasn't around, young feller."

"Y-yeah," Bush agreed, having reached the same conclusion. "He got off the first shot, Sheriff."

"I heard the two shots," Reeves replied, guessing how the youngster must be feeling. He noticed a crowd of people approaching from a civic meeting they had attended, having been attracted by the disturbance. "Now you go back inside and wait for me there."

"What has happened here, Sheriff?" a man in the forefront of the crowd demanded in an Illinois accent that had a lilt Stone thought sounded vaguely familiar.

"Some trouble, Mr. Eisteddfod," Reeves replied. "There's nothing any of you good folks can do, so I'd suggest you went about your business."

"This is the only killing we have ever had in town, look you," the man said loudly instead of heeding Reeves's words. "It will reflect badly on the way people elsewhere will think of our county."

Stone had been looking with some interest at the man he had heard was called Egbert Eustace Eisteddfod. Tall, lean, and gaunt, with sharp features and a somewhat large hooked nose, he looked more like a circuit-riding preacher for one of the lesser and more strict religious denominations than the owner of the Vertical Triple E ranch. There was no sign of a weapon anywhere about his person. On the other hand, his features had an expression that suggested he had no liking for Texans and could be using the shooting to turn the local population against them. With that in mind, Stone put to use his knowledge of the Comanche language to say something that caused the Kid to go back into the saloon.

"I haven't found out what caused it yet, Mr. Eisteddfod," Reeves stated, wondering what the boss of the Wedge had said.

"Then shouldn't you be doing it, look you?" the gaunt rancher asked. "We can't have anybody thinking killing will be condoned in Spanish Grant County."

"Nothing's been 'condoned' and never will be, so long's I wear this badge," Reeves replied coldly. He had always sensed that the man he was addressing did not approve of his appointment as sheriff.

"And that is how it should be, look you," the rancher asserted. "We have never had such a thing happen—!"

"Afore us Texans moved in?" Stone inquired, noticing that the Kid was returning accompanied by one of his hands.

Before the question was answered, Montgomerie, teetering on his heels as if far more drunk than was the case, cut loose with a flow of language that nobody gave any indication of being able to understand. Pausing for a moment, he swung on his heel and strolled into the barroom once more.

However, after doing so, he remained near the front entrance instead of continuing to the counter.

"That wasn't *said,* nor meant likely," the sheriff pointed out in his official tone, but he did not believe the second part of his declaration. Then his voice grew more authoritative and he went on in the same fashion, "So I'd be *obliged* if all you good folks'd go about your business and let me 'tend to mine."

"I was right, boss," Montgomerie declared with confidence, coming from the saloon as the crowd was dispersing. "That jasper's not Welsh no matter what he calls hisself and tries to make it sound like he is."

"How do you know?" Stone asked, and he could see Reeves listening with interest.

"Well, now, boss," the cowhand replied. "What I said in Welsh about how he looks and what he should be doing to his mother's butt end would have made him show it had he understood it."

Before any more could be said, the sounds of rapidly approaching hooves drew everybody's attention away from Montgomerie.

"Sheriff!" gasped the cowhand who came up afork a lathered horse, showing signs of having ridden fast and far. "Ed Leshin sent me in to tell you how we've found Mr. Hayes lying dead on the range with his neck bust by what looks to've been a riding accident."

"Hot damn!" Reeves breathed, reaching a conclusion from the way in which the information was worded, since he knew he and the foreman of the Arrow P ranch shared certain thoughts on the matter of recent riding accidents. "That makes *three* of them!"

"You mean that's how Uncle Cornelius Maclaine was killed?" Stone asked, not having thought to raise the subject earlier.

"And Doug Loxley of what he called the Lazy Scissors,

but has now been turned to the AW by all accounts," the sheriff supplemented. "I know coincidences happen, but this's pushing 'em further than I'm willing to stand back for. Can I take Kiowa Cotton with me to help Burt Alvord cut for sign, Stone? Because I'm going straight out there to have it done so careful comes daylight, I'll know for *certain* whether it did come off by accident this time."

"Sure," Stone assented without hesitation. "I know I didn't care much for Uncle Cornelius Maclaine, but I'll be interested to see if he got made wolf bait by accident or done deliberate."

1. How Mark Counter first made the acquaintance of Martha Jane Canary and how it developed is told in various volumes of the Floating Outfit and Calamity Jane series.

14

WE WANT THE WOMAN, SHORT STUFF!

"You wanting something, missus?" the oldest of the women employed at the Arizona State Saloon asked, having seen Steffie Willis standing outside and looking over the batwing doors.

"Can you fetch Cap'n Hart over for me?" the ash-blonde requested, aware that she must not enter the establishment and that to do so would arouse the resentment of the saloongirls.

"He's *busy* right now," replied the woman, a well rounded redhead with a dislike for females accounted "good" by the standards of the day. "Why'nt you—?"

"Either you go fetch him right now, or I'm going to do it myself," Steffie warned. She had no animosity toward members of her sex who worked in saloons, knowing the majority of them had had no other choice where obtaining employment was concerned. However, not only did she have a spirited nature that objected to such treatment, the urgent nature of the business that brought her there made her less tolerant than would otherwise have been the case. "Which I'll do it over *you* if need be."

"Why, howdy, you-all, Miz Willis, ma'am," Dusty Fog said before the redhead could reply. He had been circulating around the room and recognized the ash-blonde from the description he was once given by her husband. "If you're looking for Rusty, he's drinking, carousing, and making all kinds of fun with the ladies."

After the departure of Sheriff Amon Reeves and Kiowa Cotton—who had agreed to the request for his services as a skilled reader of sign immediately upon its being put to him—the celebrations were resumed in the saloon. Considering it a matter of priority, the small Texan and Stone Hart had first devoted their attention to helping Thorny Bush make an adjustment to the realization that he had taken another human being's life; they assured him that everybody would agree he only did so to prevent himself from being killed in a gunfight he neither sought nor wanted. They succeeded so well that the youngster was soon regaling all within hearing distance with his extensive repertoire of jokes, and on this occasion was allowed to do so without reprisals.

"Not him," Steffie was unable to prevent herself from saying despite her eagerness to see the boss of the Wedge. "He's too loyal, noble, upstanding—and scared of what I'd do to him should he do such carrying-ons to do any of 'em." Then she became serious as she continued, still remaining outside the doors. "It's Margaret."

"What about her?" Dusty asked, stepping through the front entrance.

"She's just had a letter from Mrs. Eardle asking for them to meet up secret-like to try to settle the fuss between their husbands," the ash-blonde replied. "Which she's bound 'n' determined to do, the way she's been asked. Where's Cap'n Hart?"

"He was going out to the backhouse last I saw, and isn't back yet," the small Texan answered. "Just what was she asked?"

"That she come to the meeting on her lonesome," Steffie explained. "And, knowing how set she is in her ways, I've told Becky Reeves to push her down gentle 'n' sit on her to make sure she stays put until I get back with the *other* boss."

"I surely do admire loyal and respectful help," Dusty drawled. "Look, Stone's helping the boys whoop things up to celebrate the end of the drive. Leave us let him keep on doing it and I'll come with you."

"Well—!" the ash-blonde began. However, remembering what Rusty had told her about the way a trail boss of Stone Hart's kind showed gratitude for a job well done, she decided there could be no harm in accepting the suggestion from the small Texan. From all she had heard about him—and, like the other members of the Wedge crew with whom she had spoken, her husband accorded him a respect equaled only by that given to his boss—Dusty was quite capable of dealing with any problems that might arise from following the instructions given by Mrs. Eardle. "Sure, if I can't get the *best*—!"

"I surely do admire being taken on as seconds," Dusty stated with a grin, deciding that he thoroughly approved of the obviously competent young woman his *amigo* had taken for a wife. "Let's go get her done."

"Thanks for your help, Red," Steffie called to the watching woman. "And I know I can count on *you* to keep that fool husband of mine on the straight 'n' narrow path."

Watching the curvaceously close-to-buxom and obviously sturdy ash-blonde woman walking away accompanied by the Texan—whom she, in accord with many other people who knew him, now no longer thought of as being small—the saloongirl gave a grin. Although tough in her own right, she felt as she resumed her duties that she could have been ill-advised to have caused the entrance to the saloon to be made in the manner threatened.

Dusty soon found himself being admitted to the sitting room of the sheriff's home. It was the first time he had seen Stone's wife, and as was the case with the ash-blonde, he approved of the choice made by a good friend.

"I didn't have to do what you said I should, Steffie," announced Becky Reeves, a tall and Junoesque woman in her mid-thirties who exuded the kind of rugged self-confidence that made her invaluable to her husband when he was required to deal with recalcitrant female prisoners. "But there were times when I thought it was close."

"Stone isn't with you," Margaret Hart stated, turning her head as if able to see the man who she had heard following the ash-blonde into the room.

"This's Cap'n Dusty Fog," Steffie introduced.

"Good evening, Cap'n Fog," Margaret greeted, walking forward with an assured step until she stood in front of the small Texan. Reaching forward with her right hand, she went on, "May I, please?"

"Feel free, ma'am," Dusty authorized. Then, while his face was being run over gently by the woman's fingers, he went on, "Please accept Mark's, Lon's, and my apologies for not having been able to come to your wedding."

"I do," Margaret declared with a smile, liking what her trained touch told her about the man she was examining. "Although I suspect you and those other worthless cusses who ride with you would have tried to talk him out of it."

The position of the sound of Dusty's voice told Margaret how tall he was, and her fingers formed an accurate estimate of the powerful build he possessed by touching his shoulders and biceps. Furthermore, in addition to having heard it mentioned by Stone and the permanent members of the Wedge crew—especially Rusty Willis—even though

none of them expressed it in such a fashion, she could sense
the force in his personality that made people against whom
he came in contention to suddenly feel he was far larger
than was the case.

When the situation arose, Margaret deduced correctly,
the small Texan would stand the tallest of all.

"Not me, ma'am," Dusty denied. "I reckon if I've got to
put up with taking me a wife, all my *amigos* should have to
endure it."

"I'll treat that remark with the contempt it deserves,
Dusty," Margaret claimed. "And being called 'ma'am'
makes me feel awful old."

"I'll bear it in mind, *Margaret*," the small Texan promised. "Steffie reckoned something's come up that needs a
mite more handling than you can manage being just a
woman. So, seeing's how Stone's full' occupied with making
sure those useless yahoos he calls a crew don't drink the
Arizona State dry 'n' try to haul Child City out to the edge
to save riding in so far when they want to call, I reckoned
you might be willing to let me take a hand."

"I think I can just about endure it," the tawny-haired
woman decided after a short pause to consider the proposition. Even without Steffie and Becky's objections to her
doing as was requested in the letter that had been left
attached by a thumbtack to the front door of the sheriff's
house, she had realized she would be quite ill-advised to do
so alone. Not only was she in a strange town, but she did
not have Rolf to serve as a seeing-eye dog. Furthermore,
aware of how the crew always enjoyed having their boss
with them on the celebration a trail's successful conclusion,
she had not wished to cause him to forgo it. "How much do
you know?"

"Only that you've had a letter asking you to meet up with
Mrs. Eardle in secret to see if you can come up with a way

to make your menfolk settle down peaceable," Dusty replied. "Mind if I take a look at it?"

"Feel free," Margaret authorized. "Can you fetch it, please, Steffie?"

"I already did," the ash-blonde replied, offering the small Texan a folded sheet of paper.

"Uh-huh," Dusty grunted after reading the message that contained the request of which he had been told. There were also details telling how to reach the rendezvous and a request for Mrs. Hart to come alone and without any sort of light, as it would go hard for the writer should her husband find out what she was doing. "I know you've never seen any of her writing, Margaret, but—!"

"Don't be embarrassed," the tawny-haired woman instructed with a smile. "I know what you mean, and as I'd never heard there was a Mrs. Eardle, I wouldn't be able to say whether it was her handwriting even if I could see it."

"Would you reckon as how a woman wrote it, Steffie?" the small Texan inquired, relieved that what he considered a bad *faux pas* was not regarded in such a fashion by Margaret.

"It's kind of neat for a man's hand," the ash-blonde assessed after conducting an examination of the letter. "Wouldn't you say so, Becky?"

"Yes," the sheriff's wife seconded, then she lifted the paper to her nose and sniffed it at. "Which it's a mite scented, and although we all know there're *some* who would, that doesn't strike me as being something many men would buy."

"Do you think it could be a trap of some kind, Dusty?" Steffie asked, sounding worried by the possibility even though she had already reached such a conclusion.

"It's possible," the small Texan admitted.

"Then it's *me* who's going with you, if there's any going to be done!" the ash-blonde asserted in a definite tone.

"And it's *me* Mrs. Eardle wants to meet," Margaret pointed out with an equal vehemence. "If it is a genuine request, we have to play it the way she asks, and if not— well, I doubt whether anybody around here other than we and the crew know I'm blind. Certainly those hard cases who tried to cut the herd didn't see anything to let them know."

"There likely wouldn't be that bit about you not having a light along if they had known," Dusty assessed. "And the letter would not have come."

"I'll go along with you on that and hope Stone never hears I did," Margaret declared, then swung to face the ash-blonde with an air of determination, although the way she spoke robbed the last few words of any sting. "Seeing how dark it is outside, I'll be better able to cope with it than you, Steffie. So, speaking as your *employer,* I'm stating here and now that I'm going and not you."

* * *

"Somebody's there, Dusty," Margaret Hart whispered, gesturing ahead as she and the small Texan walked together through the darkness. His eyes could barely do more than form a general idea of where they were going.

Faced with the determination shown by the tawny-haired woman, which she admitted to herself made good sense although she threatened without meaning it to quit and find a more agreeable boss, Steffie Willis had raised no further objections. Margaret, donning the cloak-coat she had brought with her for the return trip to the ranch over her gingham dress, had left the sheriff's house with Dusty Fog. As they were going through the door, Becky Reeves had said she would open the windows and, at the first hint of trouble being heard, would get word to the Arizona State Saloon as fast as Steffie could move.

At first there had been some light from the surrounding buildings to help the small Texan find the way. However, before long, Margaret and he had arrived at a part of Child City where all the premises were either closed for the night or no longer in use. The destination selected for the meeting—or site of the trap, should this prove to be the case— was a deserted and practically ruined Spanish-style mission. Although the small Texan scanned it as well as possible in the bad light, he could detect no sign of there being other humans in the vicinity. However, as they were approaching the jagged remains of a sturdy adobe exterior wall, Margaret gave the warning that there could be occupants.

"Are you here, Mrs. Eardle?" the small Texan called, bringing Margaret to a stop behind the sloping end of the wall.

"Guess again, beefhead!" a mocking masculine voice with a Northern accent replied from somewhere ahead, then snickers from several men could be heard.

"What're you fellers after?" Dusty inquired, drawing the left-side Colt Civilian Model Peacemaker revolver with his right hand while attempting to locate the men in the Stygian blackness of the night. He had tried to sound querulous at the same time and cover the sound of the hammer being cocked by speaking loudly.

"We want the woman, short stuff!" the same harsh voice replied. "Major Eardle of the AW sent us to collect her, and seeing as there's *three* of us to just the one of you, you'll save yourself a whole slew of grief if you let us have her."

"*Three* of you, huh?" Dusty said, having felt Margaret's right hand tighten a little on his left when the number was given by the speaker and a finger tap five times. "That's pretty tall odds against me, feller."

While speaking, the small Texan allowed the woman to move the direction his Colt was pointing until it was at a downward angle. When the motion stopped, he responded to a tap in the side with her other forefinger by setting free the hammer. It snapped forward, and there was a crash of detonating black powder followed by the red flare of the muzzle blast. He was dazzled by the sudden glow but cocked the single-action mechanism instinctively. While doing so, he heard a screech that was closely followed by a sound he knew to be caused by the limbs of a human being thrashing in the agony that preceded death.

Proving that Margaret had been correct in her estimation of the number of would-be captors, four revolvers were fired from different positions. All were well-aimed, but the lead struck the adobe wall and died there. Each assailant's position had been marked by a red glow, but Dusty was still too dazzled by his own shot to be able to capitalize. For a moment, the only consolation he could draw was that the vision of the trio would be just as impaired. Then he realized that there was another factor working in his favor: being blind, Margaret was oblivious to the detrimental effect caused by the muzzle flare from the weapons. What is more, as she had already proved, she could locate direction most accurately from sounds. Nor had the multiple detonations confused her.

Once again, the small Texan allowed the gentle pressure on his hand to guide its movements. He had cocked the Colt instinctively while controlling the kick of the recoil, and all was ready when he felt the same signal as before. The Peacemaker cracked, and once again, owing to his own skill and the accuracy of the guidance he had received, the detonation was followed by the sound of lead driving into human flesh and the cry of a man in mortal pain.

"He's got Purd as well as the 'breed, B—!" a startled voice claimed.

At the first word spoken, Dusty again allowed his movements to be directed by Margaret. Waiting only until he had recocked the Colt, she turned its alignment and repeated the signal. The Colt sounded. Going by the yell of alarm that rose without any suggestion of pain in it, Dusty concluded that he had made a near miss instead of inflicting injury. However, it seemed that this proved to be the last straw for the speaker.

"I'm getting the hell out of here!" the man screeched.

"And me!" announced a fresh voice redolent of equal alarm. "That son of a bitch shoots too damned straight for me!"

"They're all going who can," Margaret announced after having listened intensely to various sounds suggesting that the surviving would-be abductors were withdrawing quickly on foot.

"I'd sure like to see Steffie going lickety-split to fetch Stone and the boys along," Dusty drawled, setting the hammer of his Colt on the safety notch and returning it to its holster as leather creaked and horses were set into hurried motion. "The trouble being, there's no call for them to give up their drinking 'n' carousing and come at all."

"You know what *men* are," Margaret said, trying to control her nerves as she realized she had helped cause serious injury and probably death to two of the party lying in wait to take her captive.

"I *know* what Stone'll be when he hears what's come off," Dusty answered as the hoofbeats faded away. "*Riled* a mite, or even two mites."

                              *   *   *

The small Texan proved to be correct in his assumption.

Upon his arrival—accompanied by all his hands, the two members of Ole Devil's floating outfit, and Steffie Willis— the boss of the Wedge was in a more furious display of temper than anyone had ever seen from him. However, he calmed down a little when Margaret assured him that she was unharmed and that it was at her insistence that the small Texan had brought her to the ruined mission. Knowing how determined she could be when she decided on some line of action, Stone was willing to accept the reason he had not been informed of what was to happen. He also stated that he did not believe he could have repulsed the attackers with the skill shown by Dusty. But his anger started to rise again when he was told who had been responsible for the attempt to capture Margaret.

"By God!" the boss of the Wedge growled savagely. "Eardle's gone *way* too far this time. I'm headed—!"

"Back to the sheriff's place," Dusty interrupted. "I know those that of 'em's could took a greaser standoff, but there could be more around ready to cut in if this game fell through. They might be figuring on making another stab at it, so it's *your* place to see that it doesn't come off."

"You mean you're saying we let this damned game drop?" Stone demanded.

"Nope," the small Texan denied. "I'm going to have words with Mr. Eardle. Don't say no, *amigo*. It's better that way. Once it's over, Mark, Lon, and I'll be headed back to the OD Connected, but you're going to be making your home here. Which being, it'll be a whole heap easier if folks don't keep remembering how you let yourself get into a shooting war as soon as you got here. That Welsh feller Mont reckons isn't Welsh'd really have something to sink his teeth into."

"Dusty's making good sense, Stone," Margaret stated definitely, but could not help supplementing the assessment with "Probably for first and last time of his life." Then she went on in a tone that implied she regarded the matter as settled, "Who do you mean to have with you, Cap'n Fog?"

"Mark and Lon, for starters," the small Texan replied, giving Stone no chance to speak. "How about it, Waggles, Peaceful, Silent, are you on?"

"We've all throwed our bedrolls into Wedge's chuck wagon way back," the *segundo* answered.[1] "And they was still there last trail count."

"I just *hope* there won't be no trouble!" Peaceful Gunn wailed in his most doleful and seemingly deeply concerned fashion, as everybody expected he would.

"Just one goddamned minute, *Cap'n Fog!*" Steffie put in, stepping forward to halt with feet spread apart and arms akimbo. "Didn't you miss somebody out on your trail count?"

"I can't think who," the small Texan replied, conscious of the bitter glare that had been directed his way by Rusty Willis. "This is no chore for a married man."

"Then why're *you* going?" the ash-blonde countered. "If you reckon you're going off on this fool game without the best goddamned fighting man you've got, then you've got another thought coming."

"You in, Rusty?" Dusty asked mildly.

"My *boss* says I am," the cowhand replied.

"Got space for another hand, Cap'n?" Dude asked.

"Make that two," David Montgomerie suggested.

"I count it *three!*" Thorny Bush claimed.

"All right, 'though I'm like' to regret being so kind-hearted," Dusty assented. "Only, afore any more of you volunteer, the rest of you'll be staying out here and helping your boss ride shotgun on Mrs. Hart 'n' Mrs. Willis."

"Do it whatever way you see fit, *amigo*," Stone said, yielding to the inevitable and admitting to himself that Dusty was making good sense about Stone's not becoming actively involved. His eyes went to the Kid as he went on, "There's just one thing, though. Try to handle things without any killing, if that's possible."

---

1. *The special significance of a cowhand throwing his bedroll, which held all his most personal possessions, into a ranch's chuck wagon is explained in* TRAIL BOSS.

15

YOU DIDN'T SAVE ME FROM A LIFE OF SIN

"Looks like Mr. Eardle's expecting us coming," the Ysabel Kid reported, having returned on foot from making a reconnaissance of the AW ranch's property. "Which ain't too surprising, considering what his yahoos tried to do back in Child City."

Because of the concern that had been felt by Stone Hart over what might happen when he heard his wife went to carry out the meeting to which she was invited, he had arranged with Waggles Harrison to keep a couple of men standing near enough to the front entrance of the Arizona State Saloon to be able to hear any shooting. On being told that the boss lady could be in trouble, the members of the Wedge crew had wasted no time in collecting their horses—the animals having been calmed down by their users after Thorny Bush was compelled to defend himself against Skinny McBride—and setting off to investigate. Just as determined to find out what had happened, Steffie Willis had accompanied them on the back of her husband's mount.

Not unexpectedly, the sound of the gunplay at the ruined mission had attracted attention from some Child City citizens. However, such was the speed at which being mounted allowed Stone's group to get there that the selection of the men who were to accompany Dusty Fog in his proposed visit to the AW ranch was made before any members of the community arrived.

Carrying lanterns to supply illumination, which the Texans had not, among the first on the scene had been Counselor Edward Sutherland and the local doctor. Soon after, also bringing means of coping with the darkness, Egbert Eustace Eisteddfod had put in an appearance. He was accompanied by some of the citizens who had been with him at the civic meeting before the disturbance in front of the saloon. Though he remained in the background, on a couple of occasions he could be heard repeating his assertion that such a thing had never happened before in the town and that its future could be affected adversely. However, from what Dusty had seen, there had not seemed to be any great feelings on the subject aroused among the other citizens one way or the other.

On their way to help play a part in investigating the disturbance, the lawyer and the doctor had been informed by Becky Reeves that neither her husband nor Deputy Burt Alvord would be available to conduct an inquiry into the cause of the gunplay. On reaching the ruined mission, stating that his officially appointed position as justice of the peace required him to act in behalf of Sheriff Amon Reeves, the lawyer had set about doing so with commendable efficiency. In fact, Dusty thought he did so with a skill many a peace officer would have admired.

After ordering everybody not directly concerned to stand back and asking the doctor to examine the two shapes sprawled unmoving on the ground, Sutherland ascertained that Margaret Stone was neither injured nor in any other way distressed by what had happened. Then he asked her the reason for her being at the mission. Listening to her explanation, the small Texan was pleased by the acumen she displayed.

Margaret said she had been asked to come to the place to have a meeting with a woman who wanted to tell her something of considerable importance to herself and her husband. She told how she knew that Stone was involved in the traditional celebrations with the crew for the end of a successful trail drive and had not wanted to have him leave them. Therefore, having accepted that to go alone might be inadvisable, she agreed to allow the Rio Hondo gun wizard to accompany her. Omitting any mention of the important part she had played, she claimed that it had been entirely by Dusty's own efforts that the attempt to capture her was thwarted and two of the participants shot. Sutherland remarked that the small Texan had been fortunate enough to hit the pair fatally in the darkness, then was told that Waggles Harrison—who went with the doctor—had identified one of the pair as being among the hard cases led by Jeremy Korbin. But he disclaimed any knowledge of the other beyond assuming he was a half-breed, declared that the matter could not be taken any further until the following morning, and suggested that the crowd disperse.

Accepting what amounted to a dismissal from a man for whom the majority of them had considerable respect, the local people had shown no hesitation before taking their departure. Left with just the Texans, the doctor having gone to brief the town's undertaker, Sutherland showed his shrewd nature by requesting that he be told what had not been said so far. After hearing the full story and what was intended to be done, he had said he felt the actions justified and that he supported Stone's stipulation that there be no shooting at the AW ranch unless it was unavoidable.

Dusty and his party had experienced no particular diffi-

culty arriving in the vicinity of their destination. Calling a
halt while they were still sufficiently far from the ranch
house to prevent their presence being detected, Dusty had
sent the Kid ahead to carry out a reconnaissance and was
just receiving a report of what had been discovered.

* * *

"Sounds like the son of a bitch got word of what happened
and is fixing not to get catched out when we come looking
for evens," Thorny Bush declared in an angry tone on hearing what was said by the Ysabel Kid.

"There's something I don't cotton on to about it, Dusty,"
the black-dressed Texan asserted, paying no attention to
the youngster's outburst beyond assuming that it was
caused by anger arising from the respect he felt for Margaret. "From what I saw, none of the fellers standing watch
stack up as being paid *pistoleros*. They look 'n' act more like
saints than hired guns who know what's real likely to come
off."

"I've said all along that all the AM's I've met up with
struck me as being saints," Waggles Harrison declared, the
word "saint" used in such a context meaning an honest
cowhand. "Which being, I go along with the boss about us
doing all we can to avoid having to do any killing."

"Given Lon's right—for once in his sinful life and unlikely as it might be," Dusty Fog drawled, although certain
his very competent *amigo* had formed an accurate assessment, "there's *none* of us want any." Waiting until the
murmurs of concurrence—in which Bush joined, remembering the amiable time spent in the company of the AW's
cowhands on his first visit to Child City—died away, he
went on, "Let's hear how the land lies, so we can figure how
to play out the hand."

Using the light of a bull's-eye lantern brought along for
the purpose and a piece of ground laid bare by a bowie
knife borrowed from Peaceful Gunn, the Indian-dark

Texan produced a sketch of the layout around the ranch house and marked where each of the four guards he had located were positioned. Although the illustration did not come up to the standard a professional cartographer could have produced on a workbench, Dusty was convinced from long experience that it would be sufficiently accurate to be adequate for his needs.

Knowing their ability to perform the task, the small dusty-blond gave the duty of dealing with the guards to the Kid, Dude, Silent, and Peaceful. While they were carrying it out—in silence, if the plan was to succeed without causing blood to be spilled—the rest of the party would move in also on foot, ready to carry out the instructions they received. Listening to the way the orders were given, the *segundo* of the Wedge formed a better impression than ever of the way in which Captain Fog had performed his military duties as commanding officer of the Texas Light Cavalry's Company C during the War Between the States. Waggles concluded that if the present enterprise was not carried out as his boss required, it would not be for a lack of organization or because the men given the most important part were unable to perform in the manner called for.

"Is everybody satisfied?" Dusty asked at the conclusion of his description and, receiving a response indicating that this was so, he went on, "All right, boys, let's go get her done!"

*   *   *

It was testimony to the ability of the men selected by Dusty Fog that the subduing of the guards around the AW ranch house was accomplished in the necessary silence. Before any of them could realize the danger, much less attempt to raise an alarm, they were struck down and rendered unconscious by blows from a bowie knife's hilt or the butt of a Colt. To make sure there would be no outcry should any of them recover prematurely, each had his wrists and ankles secured by the pigging thongs, which their assailants had brought along for the purpose, and each was gagged by his own bandanna. A series of well-simulated calls such as would be made by a whippoorwill announced the completion of the task to the rest of the party, who advanced with much the same caution that had been shown by their four companions. When all were gathered close to the buildings, without further instructions they made ready to carry on with the parts assigned to them.

Leaving the remainder of the party to do as Dusty had directed, which was to take up positions from which the rest of the AW's crew could be prevented from coming out of the bunkhouse, the three members of Ole Devil's floating outfit went to play their part in the raid. Their destination the main building, they had already determined how they would effect an entrance so as to take the occupants by surprise. It was a system they had employed often enough in the past to be convinced it would serve their needs on this occasion.

Crossing the porch with silent steps, the trio halted before the front entrance. Drawing their guns and cocking the hammers, Dusty, Mark, and the Kid waited until they were sure the rest of the raiding party were ready. Satisfied upon that point, the blond giant prepared to take measures that had been decided would obtain their admittance regardless of whether or not the door was locked. Although the other two had used similar methods when their larger and heavier *amigo* had not been available, they knew he much was better equipped physically to perform the task under the prevailing conditions. Nor did either of them expect that he would fail to justify their confidence.

Swinging his right foot forward with all the power of his two-hundred-and-thirty-pound frame behind it, Mark sent its sole crashing into the door at the point where experience had taught him the impact would do most good.[1]

There was a sudden crack and the door burst inward. If the ease with which this happened was any indication, the door had not been locked. With entry obtained, the Texans went through in a way that suggested it had been learned from a well-trained peace officer. Passing the blond giant, then going to the right and left practically simultaneously, Dusty and the Kid swung their respective armament in an arc, ready to deal with any opposition. Bringing down the foot that had gained them admission, Mark followed—like the small Texan, a Colt in each hand.

There were enough indications from the bunkhouse for Waggles to conclude that the noise caused by the forced entry to the main building had been heard.

"Jimmy Conlin!" the *segundo* yelled with a volume Silent Churchman would have been hard put to beat. "This's Waggles Harrison from Wedge. We've got all the doors 'n' windows covered, so you 'n' your boys stay put and peaceable until we find out just what the hell's been going on hereabouts just recent'."

"We've got bunkies out there," the foreman of the AW replied. His voice betrayed puzzlement mingled with anxiety. "How about them?"

"None's been hurt bad," Waggles assured, realizing that a man such as he assumed Conlin to be would be concerned on that point. Then he had an inspiration and went on, "You willing to let me come in and tell you what's brought this on?"

"Come ahead and you can walk out when you've done regardless," the foreman authorized. "Because I sure as hell want to know what's coming off hereabouts."

What the *segundo* had proposed had not been part of the instructions he had received.

* * *

Looking around, Dusty Fog discovered that he and his companions had entered what must be the main dining room. Only two occupants were present—a man and a woman. Tall and burly, the man had a strong yet not hard or brutal face, close-cropped graying hair, and a military bearing that showed even though he was dressed in a civilian fashion. An expression that mixed surprise and anger came to his features as he sent his chair skidding from beneath him and started to thrust himself erect.

There was, the small Texan concluded, something vaguely familiar about the woman, who had also come to her feet. She was perhaps five feet eight in height and no longer in the first flush of youth, though there was nothing about her beautiful face to suggest how old she might be. She had blond hair in a style that was neat without being fussy. She was dressed in good clothing of a style to be expected in such a setting; the garments could not conceal a shapely figure, nor did they blatantly show it off. However, most noticeable to the small Texan was her response to the entry made by his party. Although she had begun by showing alarm, for some reason the expression appeared to be changing.

"Forget it, Wils!" the woman snapped when the man showed signs of trying to reach the Colt Peacemaker lying on top of the sidepiece. "You didn't save me from a life of sin to get me made a widow when there's no cause." Then her gaze swung toward the Texans, and she continued in a tone that came as a surprise to them, "Didn't I have enough damned trouble with you three, what with getting all those calluses on my butt riding Libby Schell's wagon and dishpan hands from helping her feed you? At least in those days you had the good manners to take your hats off when coming into a lady's presence. Well, *two* of you, anyways."

Listening to the advice given by his wife and what followed, Wilson Eardle was prey to the same emotions that were being felt by Dusty. Her reference to having been saved from a life of sin would only have been made because she knew the three Texans were aware of her past and would not hold it, or try to use it, against her. Before she married, she had worked in saloons. However, for several years her work had been in a supervisory capacity, and while she had admitted frankly before accepting his proposal that there had been other men in her life, she was not promiscuous, nor had what passed between them ever been thought by either party to be on a permanent basis. Therefore, she had not been in need of salvation from the way she made her living.

Eardle had another point to consider. The precaution of having guards posted had come about as the result of some disturbing information he had received from Child City in the afternoon. Despite the way in which the three Texans had burst in, it reminding him of the system he had seen employed by peace officers when making an entrance to a room where dangerous criminals were to be expected, there was nothing in their appearance to suggest that they had come for the reason he suspected in light of what he had been told. In fact, although their clothing was somewhat travel-stained—that of the Kid more so than the others'—they struck him as being visitors he would not have hesitated to receive had they arrived at any other time.

"Well, if this doesn't get a man all kissed off against the cushion!" Mark Counter exclaimed, staring at the woman with a look of recognition similar to that being exhibited by Dusty and the Kid. "You're April Hosman!"

"You should have been damned when you was younger, just like that no-account handsome daddy Ranse of yours who you don't feature a mite more than two peas in a pod except in the first," the woman replied, her tone and demeanor implying that she had had wide experience in dealing with men and was competent to stand on her own feet in their company. "But it's *Mrs.* April Eardle now, and that was *my* front door you booted open instead of knocking."

"I'm sorry about that, Apr—Mrs. Eardle, ma'am," Dusty declared, twirling his bone-handled guns back into their holsters. "Only, the way things looked, we thought coming in like we did was called for."

"I had some of the boys out standing guard—!" Wilson Eardle began.

"By the Lord, Dusty Fog!" April snapped, losing her air of mocking affability, but once again her gaze was mainly directed at the Kid. "If any of them are hurt—!"

"Just sore heads or jaws, at most," the small Texan asserted.

"Stone Hart told us he wanted that should be the way of it," the Kid went on with the air of one wishing to find exculpation from a false accusation. Then his voice hardened and all the amiable innocence left his Indian-dark features. "Which I thought was mighty easygoing of him after those yahoos Dusty stopped had tried to lay hold of his lady wife. There's some's'd've got more than a mite riled and uncaring about a thing like that."

"Lay hold of—?" Eardle began, his face showing a total lack of comprehension.

"I reckon this needs talking out," Dusty claimed. "Only, before we start, Mr. Eardle, I'd be obliged if you'd go tell your hands down to the bunkhouse to stay put inside, being I've told the Wedge crew to keep them there."

"Do it, Wils!" April requested, but in a tone her husband knew meant she intended to have her wish respected. "And, like I said before, you three take those hats off under my roof. I thought between us Libby Schell and I had taught you better manners than *that*."[2]

While the Texans were carrying out the order given by the blonde and her husband was preparing to carry out the request made by Dusty, they heard hurried footsteps approaching. However, as there had been no commotion from outside the building, none of them considered the matter a cause for alarm. Nor was it. Waggles and Conlin came in with a haste implying that there was something they regarded as being of the greatest importance to be imparted.

"From what Jimmy's just told me, Cap'n Fog," the *segundo* of the Wedge announced without any preliminaries, "there's a nigger in the woodpile about this whole game!"

"I was just starting to get a smidgen of a notion along those lines my own self," the Kid asserted. "There are times I'm *real* smart like that."

1. Occasions when the three members of General Ole Devil Hardin's floating outfit served as peace officers are recorded in QUIET TOWN; THE MAKING OF A LAWMAN; THE TROUBLE BUSTERS; DECISION FOR DUSTY FOG; CARDS AND COLTS; THE SMALL TEXAN; *and* THE TOWN TAMERS.
2. How the prior meeting between April Eardle, née Hosman, and the uninvited visitors to her home took place is told in .44 CALIBRE MAN.

16

THAT LEAVES JUST ONE

"You thought I held a hatred against all you Southrons over what happened to us in Arkansas during the War?" Wilson Eardle asked, running his gaze around the Texans who were seated with his wife, foreman, and himself at the dining table. "Hell—sorry, my dear—we cursed you and the rest of the Texas Light Cavalry more than once, the way you hit us, Captain Fog, but we admired you all as brave and honorable fighting men."

"And that's how we always thought of you New Jersey Dragoons, Major," the small Texan replied. "I had good cause to know it was so on a couple of occasions, at least."

After ordering the Ysabel Kid to arrange for the guards to be released and to see to it that any injuries they had sustained received treatment without delay, April Eardle, speaking in the same "accept no nonsense" fashion, had told the rest of the men in the dining room to sit down and talk things out. Then she went to the kitchen—where its Chinese occupants were engaged in a noisy game of mah-jongg that, along with the sturdy construction of the building, had prevented them from hearing the disturbance caused by the arrival of the three Texans—and gave instructions for coffee to be delivered. With this done, she had sat by her husband and listened to the raiding party as they explained what had brought them to the ranch.

Upon being informed by Waggles Harrison why the action was being taken, Jimmy Conlin had stated that there were not and never had been any *pistoleros* hired by his employer. Then he had explained that the guards had been put out because a man had arrived earlier claiming to come from Sheriff Amon Reeves with a warning that a bunch of owlhoots who were raiding in the surrounding area were reported to be headed for Spanish Grant County and that the AW Ranch would be their most likely first target. Therefore, particularly since his wife had finally joined him after having been delayed in her arrival by urgent business matters, precautions had to be taken. Hearing this, the *segundo* of the Wedge had decided that they should come to the main house immediately to help clarify the situation.

Having been assured once more that none of his guards had been seriously injured, Eardle, showing he had not forgotten the attitudes of the professional soldier, had said they deserved what happened to them for being so slack in the performance of their duties. Then, in their defense, he had suggested that they were just young cowhands who were not experienced in such matters. To further win the approbation of the Texans, he had praised those of their party responsible for the excellent way in which they had performed their duty of silencing the guards and had voiced his gratitude over the leniency they employed while doing so.

The mention by Waggles Harrison of the possible reason for Eardle's disliking Southerners had brought the incredulous response from him.

"If our *noble* veterans of the War have finished with their mutual-admiration meeting," April said in an apparently cold and disapproving fashion, "may I suggest we get on with the *important* matters that we're here to discuss."

"Were your Southern belles like *that*, Captain Fog?" Eardle inquired.

"Some of them were *worse*," Dusty answered. "Why, Belle Boyd, Mrs. Greenhow, and my cousin Betty"—at this point Mark Counter injected "and 'specially her!"—"why, they could come to being close to *terse* and even *uppity* at times."[1]

"My momma always told me the best way to make a man see reason was whomp him over the head with a skillet," April warned, realizing that the remarks just made were proof that no animosity was felt by her husband or the small Texan. "Do I have to have Hop Lee fetch one for me?"

"Anyway, gentlemen," Eardle said, "as I'm not responsible for the trouble which Captain Hart—!"

"Why not say 'Dusty' and 'Stone' instead of 'Captain,' husband of mine?" April put in, her manner redolent of badly strained patience. "There's neither of you, nor him if it comes to that, in the Army anymore—which being, I bet the Army prays every night for its good fortune."

"As I was saying, *Captain Fog*—!" the rancher began.

"I'd admire to hear it, *Major Eardley*—!" Dusty said in just as seemingly sober and serious a fashion.

"Hop Lee," April yelled. "Fetch me your *heaviest* skillet!"

"Calf rope, Miz Eardle, ma'am!" the small Texan announced, spreading his open hands in a gesture of supplication.

"I should hope so, for shame," the blonde declared, knowing the words were the way in which cowhands announced a desire to surrender. "Now, get to talking sensible, the both of you, and if any of you other knobheads—!"

"The *lady* means us three," Mark informed Waggles and Conlin as if imparting a secret of magnitude.

"Of course I do," April confirmed. "There's only my fool husband and that Rio Hondo varmint here besides you to take pick of the *remuda* from."

"I must apologize for my wife, gentlemen," Eardle said somberly, although he realized that—regardless of the gravity of the situation—he was behaving in a lighthearted fashion he had not employed since he was a young second lieutenant fresh out of West Point. He also concluded that he was finding responding in such a fashion to be enjoyable—and the cause of his wife considerable amusement. "My mother always said I was marrying beneath myself; but what did she know—look at what she had for a son. And now, unless the distaff side of the family wants to make any more frivolous interruptions, *Dusty,* seeing as how I'm not responsible for *Stone's* trouble, it strikes me as being a fairly good notion to try and find out who is."

Far from being annoyed by the reference to the statement falsely attributed by her husband to his mother, April was delighted by the way in which he was behaving like the kindhearted and considerate man she knew him to be under the mantle of hardness wrought by his military upbringing and training. They had met while he was still coming to terms with his retirement from the Army, and having recognized his true character as well as developing an affection for him equal to that he had shown her, had sought to bring it where it would be noticeable to others. It struck her now that, in the company of men like the big dusty-blond Texan she had come to respect during their meeting, he was capable of thawing out. She felt their already satisfactory life would be much improved by the change.

"I'm thinking along those same lines myself, Wils,"

Dusty admitted, employing the name April had given to her husband. "There're some who'd say the fellers who own the other two spreads hereabouts'd seem the most likely choice, and seeing that the other got himself killed in a riding accident this morning, that leaves just one."

"Going to see that one seems like the most logical way for us to find out," Eardle suggested. "And I'm willing to bet that is what you already had in mind."

"I was thinking on doing just that," the small Texan declared.

"Then some of my men and I are coming along," the rancher stated. "As there's been plenty done to make it looked like I was to blame for all the trouble Stone's been having, I want to make sure it stops happening."

"Could be we're picking on the wrong feller," Dusty reminded.

"I'm not forgetting that," Eardle replied.

"Which being, I'm going to tell Sheriff Reeves what we've found out before I do anything," Dusty warned. "Then it'll be up to him how he wants it played."

"You won't get any arguments from me on that," Eardle answered. "I haven't met him yet, but Mis—Jimmy tells me he's a decent and fair man. Only, you say there are some hired guns involved. In that case he could need help, and the stronger a posse he can take with him, the better chance he will have to deal with them."

"They do say the Good Lord is on the side of the stronger battalions," April put in, noticing with satisfaction that her husband had employed their foreman's given name instead of using "Mr. Conlin," as had been his practice previously. "And, even if it's wrong, he should be. I'll go tell Hop Lee and the rest of them to quit their game of *mah jong* and get food ready for you. My momma always said men could fight better on a full stomach and, whoever is behind this fuss will have hired guns backing him, so fighting's likely to be needed."

* * *

"Well, now, Mr. Eisteddfod," Jeremy Korbin remarked, his manner threatening. "It's time for us to be paid off so's we can be on our way."

The time was just past noon on the day after the events that had caused such a stir in Child City.

Having spent the previous day and until late at night in the town, supervising the activities of his men and creating an alibi for himself, Egbert Eustace Eisteddfod had decided to visit them instead of returning to the Vertical Triple E ranch.

Now he realized he had made an error in judgment.

Ever since he had arrived at the small yet sturdy old adobe building concealed near the center of an extensive area of woodland some eight miles from the main house of the Vertical Triple E ranch, a structure he believed was not known to exist by any members of the crew, he had been expecting something of the sort, although hoping it would come from another, less dangerous source. From the moment he had entered, he had been aware that everybody present was in a disturbed or alarmed frame of mind. Although less discernible where the surviving hired guns were concerned, Peter Medak and the young men who had been in the Arizona State Saloon were clearly frightened. Eisteddfod's instinct in such matters told him they were already making plans to get well clear of Spanish Grant County as soon as possible. The same was clearly also true of the man injured in the fight with Peaceful Gunn; this man was also present, although in no state to offer an opinion. However, knowing Korbin and his fellow *pistoleros* would pose a far greater threat to him should they desert, he had hoped they would be ruled by a desire to keep receiving their pay.

For some years before he took possession of the property he had named the Vertical Triple E ranch—using the name "Egbert Eustace Eisteddfod," selected to support his claim to be of Welsh descent—he had made a lucrative livelihood as a fence for stolen goods in Washington, D.C. As he had when circumstances compelled him to flee from the city and live in Arizona,[2] he had used an alias, "Lachlan Lachlan of McLachlan," and given Glasgow—a town in Scotland known to practically everybody with whom he had come into contact—as the place of his birth. He had adopted a suitable accent and turned to ways of living that would not be practiced by one of his true nationality in the hope that doing so would prevent the cover from being suspected.

Moving westward in his attempt to evade the law, Eisteddfod had seen a way by which he might throw any hunters off his trail completely. He had contrived to bring away most of the money acquired during his career as a fence, and this was more than sufficient for him to be able to pay his share in the scheme he had concocted with Cornelius Maclaine, Patrick Hayes, and Douglas Loxley. Obtaining the connivance of a dishonest official in the Land Office, they had purchased the four ranches into which the original Spanish grant was split on the death intestate of its owner. The arrangement was that the property of any member who died should be divided among the survivors. It had not been the most satisfactory arrangement and was the cause of considerable bitterness and hostility among the participants, although this had never been obvious to anybody other than themselves.

From the beginning, Eisteddfod had been determined that he would be the sole survivor—as he suspected was the case with the others. He did not learn until after he had arranged for the fatal accident that should have caused the C Over M to be shared by the survivors that, presumably in a fit of spite, Maclaine had left it to a nephew in Texas. Then, following a similarly created end for Loxley, he found out that the Lazy Scissors was to go to a cousin not long retired from the Army.

Determined not to be thwarted in his desire to gain possession of the whole of the former Spanish grant's lands and knowing that this could not be achieved legally—no written proof of the deal's existence having been made, for obvious reasons—Eisteddfod had started to obtain the means by which he hoped to bring it about. Having enough of the necessary connections in Arizona to know where to apply, he had secured the services of Korbin and the other hired guns. Their purpose was to create trouble between the new owners of the two ranches in such a way that each would blame the other. Because none of them had the necessary specialized knowledge to perform the task, the injured man, before being incapacitated at the hands of Peaceful Gunn, was to have hair-branded stock from both ranches in such a way as to make it appear it was being done at the instigation of either Stone Hart or Major Wilson Eardle.

Having no faith in either their intelligence or abilities, Eisteddfod had not wanted to have the six Easterners and Peter Medak foisted upon him. However, this was done at the request of a group of "liberals" with whom he had done business in Washington, D.C., and who had somehow learned of his whereabouts. Along with others of their kind in Arizona, they had no desire to see the territory status turned into states until they were sure they could take sufficient control of its affairs to be able to run things their way. Because of what was known about his past, and because he had decided it would be useful and profitable to him should they attain their ends, he had raised no objections. While far from enamored of the prospect, and despite suspecting that the men were sent in part to keep watch over him and suspecting most of them would be more of a hindrance than help, he had been unable to turn away the assistance sent to him.

By offering to accept a lower rate of pay than the others employed by Angus McTavish, claiming he wanted to gain experience at working in the West prior to taking a place of his own in another town, Medak had obtained employment as a bartender at the Arizona State Saloon. This gave him a reason for being in Child City and, when the young "liberals" were sent to take part in the causing of trouble between the two ranchers, to supervise their efforts. After the debacle of their attempt to carry out the first task assigned to them, rather than have them face a further interrogation by the shrewd sheriff Amon Reeves, Eisteddfod had ordered them to go to and remain at the place where they were staying until a means for them to return to the East could be organized.

Unlike the hired guns and the cow thief, the young "liberals" had never relished having to stay in the poorly furnished—albeit weatherproof—old Spanish house. Nor, despite their professed desire to be at one with those they considered to be of a lower status, had they cared for the disdainful way in which the older Western men had treated them. Therefore, Eisteddfod had arrived expecting them to begin demanding to be sent back to the safety of the East without delay. He had no doubt that he could deal with them easily enough. And he was confident he would be able to cope with a similar desire to leave on the part of Medak and the injured cow thief. However, he knew that what was implied by the statement from Korbin was a vastly different and infinitely more dangerous proposition.

"You've already been paid in advance for everything you've done," Eisteddfod pointed out, trying to sound less worried than he was feeling.

"Call it a parting bonus, if you like," Korbin replied.

"I don't have any money with me," Eisteddfod said in a whine.

"Then go get some from that safe you've got hid down in the cellar."

"S-safe! What *safe* is that?"

"Don't try to hand me that shit!" Korbin growled, and the other hired guns displayed a similar menacing posture. "I found it behind the junk you put there to keep it hidden almost as soon as you left us here."

"Then it must have been there since the old don's day," Eisteddfod offered.

"I might've believed you," the gambler-dressed hard case sneered. "Only, it's been opened way too recently for that, and unless it was the old son of a bitch's ghost around 'n' haunting, which don't strike me as likely, that only leaves *you* able to do the unlocking."

"I don't have the key with m—!" Eisteddfod began.

"We'll search you to make sure you aren't lying to us," Korbin threatened. "Which, should you be, we won't be any too pleased with you and'll be able to do the opening after we're through with you."

Before the matter could be taken any further, there was an interruption.

However, Eisteddfod did not regard what happened next as likely to improve his chances to any great extent.

"You in the house!" a voice yelled from the woodland surrounding the building. "This is Sheriff Amon Reeves of Spanish Grant County here. You're surrounded and best come out with your hands raised empty in the air."

---

1. *Information regarding Rose Greenhow during some of her career as a secret agent for the Confederate States is given in* MISSISSIPPI RAIDER *and* KILL DUSTY FOG!
2. *What caused Egbert Eustace Eisteddfod to leave Washington, D.C., is told in* TEXAS KIDNAPPERS.

17
WE WASN'T TOLD *THEY'D* BE
TAKING CARDS

"Well, what's it to be?" Sheriff Amon Reeves shouted after a couple of minutes had elapsed without any response from the men he was addressing. He was cupping his hands around his mouth to help increase the volume of his voice so that it could be heard more clearly in the house. "There's no way out. Are you coming peaceable, or do we use hot lead to make you?"

Aided by the skill of reading sign possessed by Kiowa Cotton and Deputy Burt Alvord, the sheriff had learned enough in the area where Patrick Hayes had died to satisfy him that no accident had been responsible for the death. Therefore, having concluded that Egbert Eustace Eisteddfod was the most likely suspect, Reeves had stated his intention of visiting the Vertical Triple E ranch to ask some searching questions. However, aware of the loyalty shown by most cowhands toward their employer—although he suspected it would not be strong in the case of the far-from-likable Welshman, as he assumed Eisteddfod to be—and wanting to avoid the possibility of trouble between the two spreads should he have Edward Leshin and some of the Arrow P crew along, he had declined the foreman's offer to accompany him and had paid the visit with just the two men he had brought from Child City.

Upon being informed of what had brought the sheriff to the ranch, and having no fondness for his employer—who was tightfisted, unsociable, and demanding to a point where he was contemplating quitting as foreman—Steven Baird had shown no hesitation over agreeing to supply information. However, before this could be done, there was a disturbance at the back of the building.

After hearing a shouted and irate demand—"What the hell do you reckon you're doing fooling with those hosses, Flunkey?"—followed by the noise of horses being disturbed, Reeves and the other three had hurried in that direction. They found a small man in a black suit of Eastern cut, whom Reeves knew to be employed by Eisteddfod as a valet, trying to catch one of the animals in the main corral. Seeing them approach, Beagle—as he had been called on the few occasions he had been seen by the sheriff accompanying the rancher in Child City—dropped the rope he was wielding inexpertly and, making a wild grab, caught the mane of a passing animal. With a surprising skill and agility, he not only bounded astride the bare back but set the horse going and made it leap over the tall rails at the far side of the enclosure.

Sent in pursuit of the departing man, Alvord returned after a time with the man's body slung over the animal's back. He claimed using a rifle bullet—which had entered through the rear of the man's skull—had been the only way the chase could be brought to an end. Baird had already told the sheriff that he was amazed at the ability shown by the valet, who had never before displayed anything of the kind and could not offer any reason for the attempt to take

flight. Although Reeves had not said so, when told that the
valet had frequently accompanied the rancher in the buck-
board that had left tracks found by Kiowa not far from the
latest supposed accident, he had concluded that the man
possessed more than just knowledge of his employer's affairs and might even have been involved in causing the
death of the two ranchers.

Showing none of the animosity that would probably have
arisen if one of the cowhands had been delivered in such a
fashion by a peace officer as little liked by them as Alvord,
Baird had continued to give the sheriff his cooperation. In
fact, he had stated he would not have thought it could have
happened in the way it had, as the valet had always professed to have no ability at riding a horse. On the other
hand, while he had disclaimed any knowledge of his employer's business other than that which applied to the daily
work to be carried out, he had stated emphatically that
there were no hired guns at the headquarters for the spread
and, with the possible exception of one who dressed as a
professional gambler and had called on a couple of occasions for some undisclosed reason, there never had been.
However, he was able to suggest a possible place for *pistoleros* to be kept without their presence becoming known.

Conscientious in the performance of his duties, Baird
had set about familiarizing himself with the terrain over
which he and the crew would be working. Stretching for
some depth beyond the stream that marked the northern
boundary of the property, the sizable area of woodland was
not marked on any of the maps of Spanish Grant County
he had seen, and he suspected it had not been mentioned
to his employer by the agent for the Land Office who arranged the sale. As he had felt sure would prove the case
when he inspected it, because longhorns preferred more-
open range, which offered better prospects for grazing and

less cover that predatory animals could use as concealment, the cattle rarely went there.

While in the woodland Baird had located the adobe house, guessed the old don who originally owned the property had kept for purposes that called for secrecy. Because he had heard Eisteddfod frequently bemoaning the lack of profit to be made from the area and threatening to rent it for use by hunters, he had decided against mentioning the discovery. He had seen a similar system operated elsewhere and found that it caused considerable trouble for the local cowhands. Therefore, aware of the kind of man for whom he was working, he believed speaking about the presence of the building would provide an added inducement for implementing the scheme.

Although Eisteddfod had never mentioned knowing of the building's existence, the foreman admitted he might have found it while riding unescorted around the range, as he often did to make sure the cowhands were not slacking in their work. If this was the case, he had said, the hired guns might be allowed to stay there so their presence in the area went unsuspected. Reeves realized that if this was so, it would supply the solution to one of the points that had been puzzling him, and he had stated his intention of carrying out an investigation.

Having spent much of his grown life as a peace officer, the sheriff had known that he would need more help than was offered by his deputy before he could put follow through on his intention. When told what Reeves had in mind, Kiowa had offered to go along; likewise, Baird told Reeves he could count on the crew of the ranch to back him. However, though he was sure he could rely upon the cowhands to stand by him, he had decided he wanted an even stronger force before attempting anything. Any *pistoleros* who were there were professional gunfighters and unlikely to yield to arrest without trying to shoot their way out.

When the situation was explained to them, the crew of the ranch agreed to accompany Reeves to Child City, where the reinforcements he regarded as essential could be obtained. Arriving in town after night had fallen, they met the men from the Wedge and the AW who had come to offer their services to the sheriff should these be needed. All too aware of the potential as fighting men of the three members of General Ole Devil Hardin's floating outfit, and knowing the rest would be worthwhile additions to his force as well, he had not hesitated before accepting their help. His force would be further strengthened by the inclusion of Counselor Edward Sutherland, who in his capacity as justice of the peace, would give added legal authority to the mission.

Aware of the difficulties that could arise while making an approach to the house holding the hired guns, Reeves had decided to leave doing so until daytime when there would be a better chance of its being accomplished successfully. The delay proved beneficial, because it allowed some other matters to be settled by the sheriff. He learned that things had been done after the party went on the visit to the AW ranch. Backed by Stone Hart's remaining men and using the authority granted by his position in the community, Sutherland conducted a search that established that none of the men responsible for the attempted abduction were still in town.

While carrying out the investigation, drawing courage from his having let it be believed that he intended to have the sheriff deputize Dusty Fog, Mark Counter, and the Ysabel Kid—all of whom were sufficiently well-known to inspire confidence—on a temporary basis, the lawyer had been told of the intimidation carried out by the hired guns, ostensibly on behalf of Major Wilson Eardle. On learning that Eardle was innocent of any wrong-doing, Sutherland concurring with the suspicions already held by the sheriff, had given instructions for Eisteddfod to be brought to him for questioning. It was discovered that the rancher had already left town, and it was assumed that he would be making for his ranch, so this would have to be delayed until after the hired guns were dealt with.

Dawn had found a grim-faced and well-armed party setting off to carry out the task of arresting the *pistoleros*.

Despite the size of the posse, such was the determination of all of its members to carry out the mission successfully that the approach and encirclement of the old house in the woodland was carried out without any alarm being raised.

When satisfied that all his men were in their assigned positions, Reeves had announced their presence.

When no answer or sign of compliance was received from the men in the building, the sheriff had repeated the demand.

Now everybody in the posse was waiting to find out what would happen next.

* * *

"The woods're full of the sons of bitches, Jer!" yelled one of the hired guns, although he had only looked through a front window.

"And there's *Dusty Fog, Mark Counter,* 'n' *the Ysabel Kid* with 'em!" another of the *pistoleros* supplemented in even greater alarm from where he was making a similar observation at the other side of the front door. "Hell's fire! We wasn't told *they'd* be taking cards in the game!"

Looking around, in addition to noticing the not-unexpected suggestion of approaching panic that was being displayed by the young Eastern "liberals," Egbert Eustace Eisteddfod could see growing alarm from all the hired guns except Jeremy Korbin; he alone of all those present was registering no emotion.

Eisteddfod had been in the West long enough to have heard the high regard cowhands always displayed when mentioning the three members of the Hardin floating outfit, and the rancher sensed that they posed an even greater threat to his existence than did the *pistoleros*. He had enough—albeit grudging—respect for the intelligence and abilities of Sheriff Amon Reeves to feel sure that his guilt in the affair was at least suspected, and he knew proof would be forthcoming if Beagle was arrested. With that in mind, he started to wonder how he might evade the consequences of what he had caused to be done and carried out himself with the aid of the dishonest jockey.

"Don't get spooked!" Korbin commanded before the rancher could arrive at any solution to the dilemma, and his tone made it clear that he was addressing the other hired guns. "*We've* got a way out. There's nothing serious they can pin on us, not even that we tried to spook some folks into not acting friendly to Stone Hart, way I did it. So all we have to do is give them this scrawny bastard here in trade for being let the hell out of the county."

"Wha–Wha—?" Eisteddfod gasped, shocked almost speechless by his sudden appreciation of what had been suggested.

"Yeah," agreed one of the men who had been in the abortive attempt to kidnap Margaret Hart. "What I've heard about Reeves, he'd sooner turn us loose like you say, Jer, than chance having some of his posse gunned down trying to take us."

"There's nothing they can pin on *me*!" the rancher snarled, having regained some of his composure. He opened his mouth to point out that not only was there no connection between them other than his being in the house—which he could claim was because he had discovered on arriving that they were using it as a hideout and was being held against his will there—but that he had an alibi for the events of the previous day.

"Like hell there's nothing," Korbin asserted before the statement could be made. "I got that flunkey of yours drunk one night and owing me money he'd lost in a poker game we was having. He allowed he could get it from you easy, seeing as how he'd helped you kill Loxley by what looked like a riding accident."

"They'll *never* believe you, and I've too much on the little bastard for him to tell on me," Eisteddfod countered desperately. "What's more, I'll tell them which of you went after the woman and who said they should do it. They'll not—!"

"You'll have to be alive afore you can tell *anything*," the gambler-dressed hired gun said quietly.

Once again realizing what was implied, Eisteddfod did not doubt that the statement he had just heard was no idle threat.

There was, the rancher knew, only one slight hope for him against the *pistoleros* plan to be set free.

Although he had never let it be known, Eisteddfod was always armed with a Remington Double Derringer carried strapped to his right wrist on a device similar to the "card hold-out" used by crooked gamblers. What was more, he had acquired an adequate proficiency in putting it to use. He decided the moment had come for him to put his ability to use. In his opinion, with Korbin dead, he would be able to compel the rest of the hard cases to do as he wanted, and they would not employ him as a means of obtaining their own escape. Having no regard for their intelligence, he was sure he could convince them that the suggestion was impractical and doomed to failure, because he would be considered an honest and influential citizen of the county and they nothing but a bunch of hired guns seeking any means to save their skins.

First, however, the rancher knew he must get rid of Korbin.

With that aim in mind, Eisteddfod began to raise his arm, giving the pressure to his right wrist that was required to cause the spring-operated mechanism of the hold-out to function.

Just an instant too late, the rancher discovered that the device upon which he was relying was not the secret he had believed it to be.

Skilled at his secondary occupation and always wary, Korbin had detected the concealed weapon on the first occasion he had met Eisteddfod and deduced how it was manipulated. Therefore, he had concluded that the rancher would be willing to use it given the need and opportunity. At the first movement that served to confirm his suppositions, he sent his right hand flashing to his conventionally holstered revolver.

Remington and Colt emerged at the same instant. Aimed at waist level and by instinctive alignment, they crashed practically in unison. Actually, it was the short-barreled concealment weapon that went off first, by what proved to be just too short a margin. Flying as directed, the .41-calibre bullet struck Korbin between the eyes. Despite being killed instantaneously, a death spasm from Korbin discharged the revolver and its lead ripped into the rancher's heart.

The detonations came just after the sheriff had shouted his second demand for surrender. Watching as the bodies of their leaders went down, the other men present were filled with an even greater perturbation. It only needed one of the *pistoleros* to throw down his revolver and state an intention of going to obey the order for the rest to follow suit. Nor were the "liberals," Peter Medak, and the intended hair-brander any slower to comply. Yelling for the posse not to open fire and making sure their hands were raised above their heads, they all made efforts to be the first to leave the building.

"Well, Stone," Major Wilson Eardle said on discovering what had happened to Eisteddfod and Korbin. "I reckon we can say it's *over*!"[1]

"Why, sure," the boss of the Wedge—which was now a ranch and not a bunch of trail drivers working on contract—replied. "There's one thing, though."

"What would that be?" the owner of the AW inquired.

"Unless they've been left to somebody in a will," Stone said with a grin, "there're two spreads hereabouts going to be put up for sale. Why don't you and me bid for one apiece?"

"That's not a bad notion, for a Johnny Reb," Eardle asserted, but the use of the name given to a supporter of the Confederate cause had no sting. "Going by what's happened since we got here, a feller should be choosy in who he has for neighbors."

"That's the first time I ever heard a Yankee make good sense," Stone declared.

"And I go along with you all the way now Wedge has come home."

1. *That peace had not come to Spanish Grant County is proved in* ARIZONA RANGE WAR *and* ARIZONA GUN LAW.

APPENDIX ONE

By the time he reached the age of seventeen, following his enrollment in the Army of the Confederate States,[1] Dustine Edward Marsden "Dusty" Fog had won a promotion in the field to the rank of captain and was put in command of Company C, Texas Light Cavalry.[2] At the head of it, throughout the campaign in Arkansas, he had earned the reputation for being an exceptional military raider and worthy contemporary of Turner Ashby and John Singleton "the Gray Ghost" Mosby, the South's other leading exponents of what would later become known as "commando" raids.[3] In addition to averting a scheme by a Union general to employ a virulent version of what was later to be given the name, "mustard gas" (used by the Germans in World War 1)[4] and preventing a pair of pro-Northern fanatics from starting an Indian uprising that would have decimated much of Texas,[5] he had supported Belle "the Rebel Spy" Boyd on two of her most dangerous assignments.[6]

At the conclusion of the War Between the States, Dusty became the *segundo* of the great OD Connected ranch in Rio Hondo County, Texas. Its brand was a letter *O* to which was attached a *D*. Its owner and his maternal uncle, General Jackson Baines "Ole Devil" Hardin, C.S.A., had been crippled in a riding accident and was confined to a wheelchair.[7] This placed much responsibility, including the need to handle an important mission—with the future relationship between the United States and Mexico at stake—upon his young shoulders.[8] While carrying out the assignment, he met Mark Counter and the Ysabel Kid. Not only did they do much to bring it to a successful conclusion, they became his closest friends and leading lights of the ranch's floating outfit.[9] After helping to gather horses to replenish the ranch's depleted *remuda*,[10] he was sent to assist Colonel Charles Goodnight[11] on the trail drive to Fort Sumner, New Mexico, which did much to help Texas recover from the impoverished conditions left by the war.[12] With that achieved, he had been equally successful in helping Goodnight convince other ranchers it would be possible to drive large herds of longhorn cattle to the railroad in Kansas.[13]

Having proven himself to be a first class cowhand, Dusty went on to become acknowledged as a very competent trail boss,[14] roundup captain,[15] and town-taming lawman.[16] Competing in the first Cochise County Fair in Arizona, against a number of well-known exponents of very rapid drawing and accurate shooting with revolvers, he won the title, "The Fastest Gun in the West."[17] In later years, following his marriage to Lady Winifred Amelia "Freddie Woods" Besgrove-Woodstole,[18] he became a noted diplomat.

Dusty never found his lack of stature an impediment to his achievements. In fact, he occasionally found it helped him to achieve a purpose.[19] To supplement his natural strength,[20] also perhaps with a desire to distract attention from his small size, he had taught himself to be completely ambidextrous.[21] Possessing perfectly attuned reflexes, he could draw either, or both, his Colts—whether the 1860 army model,[22] or its improved descendant, the fabled 1873 model Peacemaker[23]—with lightning speed and shoot most accurately. Furthermore, Ole Devil Hardin's valet, Tommy Okasi, was Japanese and a trained samurai warrior.[24] From him, as was the case with the general's "granddaughter," Elizabeth "Betty" Hardin,[25] Dusty learned jujitsu and karate. Neither form of unarmed combat had received the publicity it would be given in later years and was little known in the Western Hemisphere at that time. Therefore, Dusty found the knowledge useful when he had to fight with bare hands against larger, heavier, and stronger men.

1. Details of some of Dustine Edward Marsden "Dusty" Fog's activities prior to his enrollment are given in Part Five, "A Time for Improvisation, Mr. Blaze," J.T.'S HUNDREDTH.

2. Told in YOU'RE IN COMMAND NOW, MR. FOG.

3. Told in THE BIG GUN, UNDER THE STARS AND BARS, Part One, "The Futility of War," THE FASTEST GUN IN TEXAS *and* KILL DUSTY FOG!

4. Told in A MATTER OF HONOR.

5. Told in THE DEVIL GUN.

6. Told in THE COLT AND THE SABER *and* THE REBEL SPY.

6a. More details of the career of Belle "the Rebel Spy" Boyd can be found in MISSISSIPPI RAIDER; BLOODY BORDER; TRIGGER MASTER; RENEGADE—THE HOODED RIDERS; THE BAD BUNCH; SET A-FOOT; TO ARMS! TO ARMS! IN DIXIE!; THE SOUTH WILL RISE AGAIN; THE QUEST FOR BOWIE'S BLADE; Part Eight, "Affair of Honor," J.T.'S HUNDREDTH *and* Part Five, "The Butcher's Fiery End," J.T.'S LADIES.

7. Told in Part Three, "The Paint," THE FASTEST GUN IN TEXAS.

7a. Further information about the general's earlier career is given in the Ole Devil Hardin and Civil War series. His death is recorded in DOC LEROY, M.D.

8. Told in THE YSABEL KID.

9. "Floating Outfit": a group of four to six cowhands employed by a large ranch to work the more distant sections of the property. Taking food in a chuck wagon, or "greasy sack" on the back of a mule, they would be away from the ranch house for long periods and so were selected for their honesty, loyalty, reliability, and capability in all aspects of their work. Because of General Hardin's prominence in the affairs of Texas, the OD Connected's floating outfit was frequently sent to assist such of his friends who found themselves in difficulties or endangered.

10. Told in .44 CALIBRE MAN *and* A HORSE CALLED MOGOLLON.

11. Rancher and master cattleman Charles Goodnight never served in the army. The rank was honorary and granted by his fellow Texans in respect for his abilities as a fighting man and leader.

11a. In addition to playing an active part in the events recorded in the books referred to in Footnotes 13 and 14, Colonel Goodnight makes guest appearances in Part One, "The Half Breed," THE HALF BREED; *its expansion,* WHITE INDIANS *and* IS-A-MAN.

11b. Although Dusty Fog never received higher official rank than captain, in the later years of his life, he, too, was given the honorific, "Colonel" for possessing the same qualities.

12. Told in GOODNIGHT'S DREAM—*Bantam Books, U.S.A., July 1974 edition re-titled,* THE FLOATING OUTFIT, *despite our already having had a volume of that name published by Corgi Books, U.K., see Footnote 19—and* FROM HIDE AND HORN.

13. Told in SET TEXAS BACK ON HER FEET—*although Berkley Books, New York, re-titled their October 1978 edition* VIRIDIAN'S TRAIL, *they reverted to the original title when re-issuing the book in July 1980—and* THE HIDE AND TALLOW MEN.

14. Told in TRAIL BOSS.

15. Told in THE MAN FROM TEXAS.

16. Told in QUIET TOWN; THE MAKING OF A LAWMAN; THE TROUBLE BUSTERS; DECISION FOR DUSTY FOG; CARDS AND COLTS; THE CODE OF DUSTY FOG; THE GENTLE GIANT; THE SMALL TEXAN *and* THE TOWN TAMERS.

17. Told in GUN WIZARD.

18. Lady Winifred Besgrove-Woodstole appears as "Freddie Woods" in THE TROUBLE BUSTERS; THE MAKING OF A LAWMAN; THE GENTLE GIANT; BUFFALO ARE COMING!; THE FORTUNE HUNTERS; WHITE STALLION, RED MARE; THE WHIP AND THE WAR LANCE *and* Part Five, "The Butcher's Fiery End," J.T.'S LADIES. *She also guest stars under her married name, Mrs. Freddie Fog, in* NO FINGER ON THE TRIGGER *and* CURE THE TEXAS FEVER.

19. Three occasions when Dusty Fog utilized his small size to his advantage are described in KILL DUSTY FOG!; Part One, "Dusty Fog and the Schoolteacher," THE HARD RIDERS; *its expansion,* TRIGGER MASTER; *and* Part One, "The Phantom of Gallup Creek," THE FLOATING OUTFIT.

20. Two examples of how Dusty Fog exploited his exceptional physical strength are given in MASTER OF TRIGGERNOMETRY *and* THE PEACEMAKERS.

21. The ambidextrous prowess was in part hereditary. It was possessed and exploited with equal success by Freddie and Dusty's grandson, Alvin Dustine "Cap" Fog who also inherited his grandfather's physique of a Hercules in miniature. Alvin utilized these traits to help him be acknowledged as one of the finest combat pistol shots in the United States during the Prohibition era and to earn his nickname by becoming the youngest man ever to hold the rank of captain in the Texas Rangers. See the Alvin Dustine "Cap" Fog series for further details of his career.

22. Although the military sometimes claimed derisively it was easier to kill a sailor than a soldier, the weight factor of the respective weapons had caused the United States Navy to adopt a revolver of .36 caliber while the army employed the larger .44. The reason was that the weapon would be carried on a seaman's belt and not—handguns having been originally and primarily developed for use by cavalry—on the person or saddle of a man who would be doing most of his traveling and fighting from the back of a horse. Therefore, .44 became known as the "army" caliber and .36, the "navy."

23. Details about the Colt model of 1873, more frequently known as the Peacemaker, can be found in those volumes following THE PEACEMAK-ERS *on our list of titles in chronological sequence for the Floating Outfit series.*

24. "Tommy Okasi" is an Americanized corruption of the name given by the man in question, who had left Japan for reasons which the Hardin, Fog, and Blaze families refuse to divulge even at this late date, when he was rescued from a derelict vessel in the China Sea by a ship under the command of General Hardin's father.

25. The same members of the Hardin, Fog, and Blaze families cannot—or will not—make any statement about the exact relationship between Elizabeth "Betty" and her "grandfather" General Hardin.

25a. Betty Hardin appears in Part Five, "A Time for Improvisation, Mr. Blaze," J.T.'S HUNDREDTH; Part Four, "It's Our Turn to Improvise, Miss Blaze," J.T.'S LADIES; KILL DUSTY FOG!; THE BAD BUNCH; McGRAW'S INHERITANCE; TRIGGER MASTER; Part Two, "The Quartet," THE HALF BREED; *its expansion* TEXAS KIDNAPPERS; THE RIO HONDO WAR; GUNSMOKE THUNDER *and* CURE THE TEXAS FEVER.

APPENDIX TWO

WITH his exceptional good looks and magnificent physical development,[1] Mark Counter presented the kind of appearance many people expected of a man with the reputation gained by his *amigo,* Captain Dustine Edward Marsden "Dusty" Fog. It was a fact of which they took advantage when the need arose.[2] On one occasion, it was also the cause of the blond giant being subjected to a murder attempt although the Rio Hondo gun wizard was the intended victim.[3]

While serving as a lieutenant under the command of General Bushrod Sheldon in the War Between the States, Mark's merits as an efficient and courageous officer had been overshadowed by his unconventional taste in uniforms. Always something of a dandy, coming from a wealthy family had allowed him to indulge his whims. Despite considerable opposition and disapproval from hidebound senior officers, his adoption of a "skirtless" tunic in particular had come to be much copied by the other rich young bloods of the Confederate States Army.[4] Similarly in later years, having received an independent income through the will of a maiden aunt,[5] his taste in attire had dictated what the well dressed cowhand from Texas would wear to be in fashion.

When peace had come between the North and the South, Mark had accompanied Sheldon to fight for Emperor Maximilian in Mexico. There he had met Dusty Fog and the Ysabel Kid. On returning with them to Texas, he had received an offer to join the floating outfit of the OD Connected ranch. Knowing his two older brothers could help his father, Big Ranse, to run the family's R over C ranch in the Big Bend country—and considering life would be more enjoyable and exciting in the company of his two *amigos*—he accepted.

An expert cowhand, Mark had become known as Dusty's right bower.[6] He had also gained acclaim by virtue of his enormous strength. Among other feats, it was told how used a tree trunk in the style of a Scottish caber to dislodge outlaws from a cabin in which they had forted up,[7] and broke the neck of a Texas longhorn steer with his bare hands.[8] He had acquired further fame for his ability at bare-handed roughhouse brawling. However, due to spending so much time in the company of the Rio Hondo gun wizard, his full potential as a gunfighter received little attention. Nevertheless, men who were competent to judge such matters stated that he was second only to the small Texan when it came to drawing fast and shooting accurately with a brace of long barreled Colt revolvers.[9]

Many women found Mark irresistible, including Martha "Calamity Jane" Canary.[10] However, in his younger days, only one—the lady outlaw,

Belle Starr—held his heart.[11] It was not until several years after her death that he courted and married Dawn Sutherland, whom he had first met on the trail drive taken by Colonel Charles Goodnight to Fort Sumner, New Mexico.[12] The discovery of oil on their ranch brought added wealth to them, and this commodity now forms the major part of the present family members' income.[13]

Recent biographical details we have received from the current head of the family, Andrew Mark "Big Andy" Counter, establish that Mark was descended on his mother's side from Sir Reginald Front de Boeuf, notorious as lord of Torquilstone Castle in Medieval England[14] and who lived up to the family motto, *Cave Adsum.*[15] However, although a maternal aunt and her son, Jessica and Trudeau Front de Boeuf, behaved in a way that suggested they had done so,[16] the blond giant had not inherited the very unsavory character and behavior of his ancestor.

1. Two of Mark Counter's grandsons, Andrew Mark "Big Andy" Counter and Ranse Smith inherited his good looks and exceptional physique as did two great-grandsons, Deputy Sheriff Bradford "Brad" Counter and James Allenvale "Bunduki" Gunn. Unfortunately, while willing to supply information about other members of his family, past and present, "Big Andy" has so far declined to allow publication of any of his own adventures.

1a. Some details of Ranse Smith's career as a peace officer during the Prohibition era are recorded in THE JUSTICE OF COMPANY Z, THE RETURN OF RAPIDO CLINT AND MR. J. G. REEDER *and* RAPIDO CLINT STRIKES BACK.

1b. Brad Counter's activities are described in Part Eleven, "Preventive Law Enforcement," J.T.'S HUNDREDTH *and the Rockabye County series, covering aspects of law enforcement in present day Texas.*

1c. Some of James Gunn's life story is told in Part Twelve, "The Mohawi's Powers," J.T.'S HUNDREDTH *and the Bunduki series. His nickname arose from the Swahili word for a handheld firearm of any kind being "bunduki" and gave rise to the horrible pun that when he was a child he was, "Toto ya Bunduki," meaning, "son of a gun."*

2. One occasion is recorded in THE SOUTH WILL RISE AGAIN.

3. The incident is described in TEXAS ASSASSIN.

4. The Manual of Dress Regulations for the Confederate States Army stipulated that the tunic should have "a skirt extending halfway between hip and knee."

5. The legacy also caused two attempts to be made upon Mark's life, see CUT ONE, THEY ALL BLEED *and Part Two, "We Hang Horse Thieves High,"* J.T.'S HUNDREDTH.

6. "Right bower"; second in command, derived from the name given to the second highest trump card in the game of euchre.

7. Told in RANGELAND HERCULES.

8. *Told in* THE MAN FROM TEXAS, *this is a rather "pin-the-tail-on-the-donkey" title used by our first publishers to replace our own,* ROUNDUP CAPTAIN, *which we considered far more apt.*

9. *Evidence of Mark Counter's competence as a gunfighter and his standing compared to Dusty Fog is given in* GUN WIZARD.

10. *Martha "Calamity Jane" Canary's meetings with Mark Counter are described in* Part One, "The Bounty on Belle Starr's Scalp," TROUBLED RANGE; *its expansion,* TEXAS TRIO; Part One, "Better Than Calamity," THE WILDCATS; *its expansion,* CUT ONE, THEY ALL BLEED; THE BAD BUNCH; THE FORTUNE HUNTERS; THE BIG HUNT *and* GUNS IN THE NIGHT.

10a. *Further details about the career of Martha Jane Canary are given in the Calamity Jane series, also;* Part Seven, "Deadwood, August the 2nd, 1876," J.T.'S HUNDREDTH; Part Six, "Mrs. Wild Bill," J.T.'S LADIES *and she makes a guest appearance in* Part Two, "A Wife for Dusty Fog," THE SMALL TEXAN.

11. *How Mark Counter's romance with Belle Starr commenced, progressed, and ended is told in* Part One, "The Bounty on Belle Starr's Scalp," TROUBLED RANGE; *its expansion,* TEXAS TRIO; THE BAD BUNCH; RANGELAND HERCULES; THE CODE OF DUSTY FOG; Part Two, "We Hang Horse Thieves High," J.T.'S HUNDREDTH; THE GENTLE GIANT; Part Four, "A Lady Known as Belle," THE HARD RIDERS *and* GUNS IN THE NIGHT.

11a. *Belle Starr "stars"—no pun intended—in* CARDS AND COLTS; Part Four, "Draw Poker's Such a *Simple* Game," J.T.'S LADIES RIDE AGAIN *and* WANTED! BELLE STARR.

11b. *She also makes guest appearances in* THE QUEST FOR BOWIE'S BLADE; Part One, "The Set-Up," SAGEBRUSH SLEUTH; *its expansion,* WACO'S BADGE *and* Part Six, "Mrs. Wild Bill," J.T.'S LADIES.

11c. *We are frequently asked why it is the "Belle Starr" we describe is so different from a photograph that appears in various books. The research of the world's foremost fictionist genealogist, Philip Jose Farmer—author of, among numerous other works,* TARZAN ALIVE, *A Definitive Biography of Lord Greystoke and* DOC SAVAGE, *His Apocalyptic Life—with whom we consulted, have established the lady about whom we are writing is not the same person as another equally famous bearer of the name. However, the Counter family have asked Mr. Farmer and ourselves to keep her true identity a secret and this we intend to do.*

12. *Told in* GOODNIGHT'S DREAM *and* FROM HIDE AND HORN.

13. *This is established by inference in* Case Three, "The Deadly Ghost," ALVIN FOG, TEXAS RANGER.

14. *See:* IVANHOE, *by Sir Walter Scott.*

15. *"Cave Adsum"; roughly translated from Latin, "Beware, I am Here."*

16. *Some information about Jessica and Trudeau Front de Boeuf can be found in* CUT ONE, THEY ALL BLEED; Part Three, "Responsibility to Kinfolks," OLE DEVIL'S HANDS AND FEET *and* Part Four, "The Penalty of False Arrest," MARK COUNTER'S KIN.

APPENDIX THREE

RAVEN HEAD, only daughter of Chief Long Walker, war leader of the *Pehnane*—Wasp, Quick Stinger, Raider—Comanche's Dog Soldier lodge and his French Creole *pairaivo*,[1] married an Irish-Kentuckian adventurer, Big Sam Ysabel, but died giving birth to their first child.

Baptized Loncey Dalton Ysabel, the boy was raised after the fashion of the *Nemenuh*.[2] With his father away from the camp for much of the time, engaged in the family's combined businesses of mustanging—catching and breaking wild horses[3]—and smuggling, his education had largely been left in the hands of his maternal grandfather.[4] From Long Walker, he learned all those things a Comanche warrior must know: how to ride the wildest freshly caught mustang, or make a trained animal subservient to his will while "raiding"—a polite name for the favorite pastime of the male *Nemenuh*, stealing horses—to follow the faintest tracks and just as effectively conceal signs of his own passing;[5] to locate hidden enemies, or keep out of sight himself when the need arose; to move in silence on the darkest of nights, or through the thickest cover; to know the ways of wild creatures[6] and, in some cases, imitate their calls so well that others of their kind were fooled.[7]

The boy proved a most excellent pupil at all the subjects. Nor were practical means of protecting himself forgotten. Not only did he learn to use all the traditional weapons of the Comanche,[8] when he had come into the possession of firearms, he had inherited his father's Kentuckian skill at shooting with a rifle and, while not *real* fast on the draw—taking slightly over a second to bring his Colt second model of the 1848 Dragoon revolver and fire, whereas a top hand could practically halve that time—he could perform passably with it. Furthermore, he won his *Nemenuh* "man-name," *Cuchillo*, Spanish for knife, by his exceptional ability at wielding one. In fact, it was claimed, by those best qualified to judge, that he could equal the alleged designer in performing with the massive and special type of blade that bore the name of Colonel James Bowie.[9]

Joining his father in smuggling expeditions along the Rio Grande, the boy became known to the Mexicans of the border country as *Cabrito*—the Spanish name for a young goat—a nickname which arose out of hearing white men refer to him as the Ysabel Kid, but it was spoken *very* respectfully in that context. Smuggling was not an occupation to attract the meek and mild of manner, yet even the roughest and toughest of the bloody border's denizens came to acknowledge it did not pay to rile up Big Sam Ysabel's son. The education received by the Kid had not been calculated to develop any over-inflated belief in the sanctity of human life. When crossed, he dealt with the situation like a *Pehnane* Dog Soldier—to which war lodge of savage and *most* efficient warriors he had earned initiation—swiftly and in an effectively deadly manner.

During the War Between the States, the Kid and his father rode as scouts for Colonel John Singleton "the Gray Ghost" Mosby. Soon, however, their specialized knowledge and talents were diverted to having them collect and deliver to the Confederate States authorities in Texas, supplies that had been purchased in Mexico, or run through the blockade by the United States Navy into Matamoros. It was hard and dangerous work,[10] but never more so than the two occasions when they became engaged in assignments with Belle "the Rebel Spy" Boyd.[11]

Soon after the war ended, Sam Ysabel was murdered. While hunting down the killers, the Kid met Captain Dustine Edward Marsden "Dusty" Fog and Mark Counter. When the mission upon which they were engaged was brought to its successful conclusion, learning the Kid no longer wished to go on either smuggling or mustanging, the small Texan offered him employment at the OD Connected ranch. It had been in the capacity as scout rather than ordinary cowhand that he was employed, and his talents in that field were frequently of the greatest use as a member of the floating outfit.

The acceptance of the job by the Kid was of the greatest benefit all around. Dusty acquired another loyal friend who was ready to stick with him through any kind of peril. The ranch obtained the services of an extremely capable and efficient fighting man. For his part, the Kid was turned from a life of petty crime—with the ever present danger of having his illicit activities develop into serious law-breaking—and became a useful and law abiding member of society. Peace officers and honest citizens might have found cause to feel grateful for that. His *Nemenuh* upbringing would have made him a terrible and murderous outlaw if he had been driven into a life of violent crime.

Obtaining his first repeating rifle—a Winchester 1866 model, although at first known as the "New Improved Henry," nicknamed the "Old Yellowboy" because of its brass frame—while in Mexico with Dusty and Mark, the Kid had soon become an expert in its use. At the First Cochise County Fair in Arizona, despite circumstances compelling him to use a weapon with which he was not familiar,[12] he won first prize in the rifle-shooting competition against stiff opposition. The prize was one of the legendary Winchester rifle models of 1873, which qualified for the honored designation, "One of a Thousand."[13]

It was, in part, through the efforts of the Kid that the majority of the Comanche bands agreed to go onto the reservation, following attempts to ruin the signing of the treaty.[14] It was to a large extent because of his efforts that the outlaw town of Hell was located and destroyed.[15] Aided by Annie "Is-A-Man" Singing Bear—a girl of mixed parentage who gained the distinction of becoming accepted as a *Nemenuh* warrior[16]—he played a major part in preventing the attempted theft of Morton Lewis's ranch, provoking trouble with the *Kweharehnuh* Comanche.[17] To help a young man out of difficulties caused by a gang of card cheats, he teamed up with the lady outlaw, Belle Starr.[18] When he accompanied Martha "Calamity Jane" Canary to inspect a ranch she had inherited, they became involved in as dangerous a situation as either had ever faced.[19]

Remaining at the OD Connected ranch until he, Dusty, and Mark met their deaths while on a hunting trip to Kenya shortly after the turn of the century, his descendants continued to be associated with the Hardin, Fog, and Blaze clan and the Counter family.[20]

1. "Pairaivo": *first, or favorite wife. As is the case with the other Comanche terms, this is a phonetic spelling.*

2. "Nemenuh"; *"the people," the Comanches' name for themselves and their nation. Members of other tribes with whom they came into contact called them, frequently with good cause, the "Tshaoh," the "enemy people."*

3. *A description of the way in which mustangers operated is given in* .44 CALIBRE MAN *and* A HORSE CALLED MOGOLLON.

4. *Told in* COMANCHE.

5. *An example of how the Ysabel Kid could conceal his tracks is given in* Part One, "The Half Breed," THE HALF BREED.

6. *Two examples of how the Ysabel Kid's knowledge of wild animals was turned to good use are given in* OLD MOCCASINS ON THE TRAIL *and* BUFFALO ARE COMING!

7. *An example of how well the Ysabel Kid could impersonate the call of a wild animal is recorded in* Part Three, "A Wolf's a Knowing Critter," J.T.'S HUNDREDTH.

8. *One occasion when the Ysabel Kid employed his skill with traditional Comanche weapons is described in* RIO GUNS.

9. *Some researchers claim that the actual designer of the knife which became permanently attached to Colonel James Bowie's name was his oldest brother, Rezin Pleasant. Although it is generally conceded the maker was James Black, a master cutler in Arkansas, some authorities state it was manufactured by Jesse Cliffe, a white blacksmith employed by the Bowie family on their plantation in Rapides Parish, Louisiana.*

9a. *What happened to James Bowie's knife after his death in the final assault of the siege of the Alamo Mission, San Antonio de Bexar, Texas, on March the 6th, 1836, is told in* GET URREA *and* THE QUEST FOR BOWIE'S BLADE.

9b. *As all James Black's knives were custom made, there were variations in their dimensions. The specimen owned by the Ysabel Kid had a blade eleven and a half inches in length, two and a half inches wide, and a quarter of an inch thick at the guard. According to William "Bo" Randall, of Randall-*

Made Knives, Orlando, Florida—a master cutler and authority on the subject in his own right—James Bowie's knife weighed forty-three ounces, having a blade eleven inches long, two and a quarter inches wide, and three-eighths of an inch thick. His company's Model 12 "Smithsonian" Bowie knife—one of which is owned by James Allenvale "Bunduki" Gunn, details of whose career can be found in the Bunduki series—is modeled on it.

9c. One thing all bowie knives have in common, regardless of dimensions, is a clip point. The otherwise unsharpened back of the blade joins and becomes an extension of the main cutting surface in a concave arc, whereas a spear point—which is less utilitarian—is formed by the two sides coming together in symmetrical curves.

10. An occasion when Big Sam Ysabel went on a mission without his son is recorded in THE DEVIL GUN.

11. Told in BLOODY BORDER *and* RENEGADE.

12. The circumstances are described in GUN WIZARD.

13. When manufacturing the extremely popular Winchester rifle model of 1873—which they claimed to be the "Gun That Won the West"—the makers selected all those barrels found to shoot with exceptional accuracy to be fitted with set triggers and given a special fine finish. Originally, these were inscribed, "1 of 1,000," but this was later changed to script, "One of a Thousand." However, the title was a considerable understatement. Only one hundred and thirty-six out of a total production of 720,610 qualified for the distinction. Those of a grade lower were to be designated, "One of a Hundred," but only seven were so named. The practice began in 1875 and was discontinued three years later because the management decided it was not good sales policy to suggest different grades of gun were being produced.

14. Told in SIDEWINDER.

15. Told in HELL IN THE PALO DURO *and* GO BACK TO HELL.

16. How Annie Singing Bear acquired the distinction of becoming a warrior and won her "man-name" is told in IS-A-MAN.

17. Told in WHITE INDIANS.

18. Told in Part Two, "The Poison and the Cure," WANTED! BELLE STARR.

19. Told in WHITE STALLION, RED MARE.

20. Mark Scrapton, a grandson of the Ysabel Kid, served as a member of Company "Z," Texas Rangers, with Alvin Dustine "Cap" Fog and Ranse Smith—respectively grandsons of Captain Dustine Edward Marsden "Dusty" Fog and Mark Counter—during the Prohibition era. Information about their specialized duties is recorded in the Alvin Dustine "Cap" Fog series.